"Billy, I . . . I don't know what to say."

"Say you love me," he said in a low voice. "Say that you'll be there for me."

"I do love you," Carrie insisted. "I love you so much. . . ."

"When you love someone, sometimes you have to make tough decisions."

Carrie bit her lip. "If it were all reversed, would you give up everything to follow me to New Jersey?"

Billy blinked for a moment. "I hope so," he finally said. He looked out the window.

"I can't tell you what to do, Car. But I can tell you how much it would mean to me if you came with me."

Carrie waited a long time before she said anything. And finally she told Billy the truth.

"I'm not sure," she whispered. "I'm just not sure."

Which left them exactly nowhere.

D1570788

Sunset Tears

CHERIE BENNETT

Sunset™
Island

SPLASH™

A BERKLEY / SPLASH BOOK

SUNSET TEARS is an original publication of
The Berkley Publishing Group.
This work has never appeared before in book form.

SUNSET TEARS

A Berkley Book / published by arrangement with
General Licensing Company, Inc.

PRINTING HISTORY
Berkley edition / August 1995

A GLC BOOK

Splash and *Sunset Island* are trademarks belonging to
General Licensing Company, Inc.

ISBN: 0-425-15027-5

BERKLEY®
Berkley Books are published by
The Berkley Publishing Group,
200 Madison Avenue, New York, New York 10016.
BERKLEY and the "B" design
are trademarks belonging to Berkley Publishing Corporation.

PRINTED IN THE UNITED STATES OF AMERICA

10 9 8 7 6 5 4 3 2 1

For the Pres in my life

Sunset Tears

ONE

"Ah, yes," Samantha Bridges intoned dramatically, closing her eyes tightly and waving her arms around as a fortune teller would over a crystal ball. "I am Sam Bridges, psychic to the stars. I know all and I tell all—for a small fee, of course. Right now, I see . . . I see . . ."

"See what, O psychic one?" Emma Cresswell asked in a teasing voice.

"I see Carrie Alden with Billy Sampson," Sam declared meaningfully.

"I like the sound of that," Carrie said wistfully.

"What exactly are they doing?" Emma prompted.

"Whoa, baby!" Sam exclaimed, a stunned look on her face. "This is so hot! I see Billy

1

with his manly arms wrapped tightly around her. She's kissing him passionately. Now I'm seeing a room—a bedroom! It's pure white, and—"

"Stop it!" Carrie Alden protested good-naturedly, tugging gently on a lock of Sam's wild red hair. "Just cut it out."

"You love it," Sam teased her.

"Come on," Carrie said, "get out your money. We're gonna get some *real* psychic advice now."

"What, you don't believe I know all and tell all?" Sam asked, wide-eyed.

"Nope," Carrie said with a laugh. "Not that you don't come up with some great gossip now and then, though."

"I really don't believe in this psychic stuff," Emma said skeptically.

"Me neither," said Carrie, grinning, "but with a psychic fair right here on the island, how could we miss it?"

"Easy," Sam replied. "We could be out with our mega-fine boyfriends doing what comes naturally. Instead we're about to let weirdos pretend they can see into our future."

"Be open-minded," Carrie said playfully.

"This is something you've never done before—you told me so yourself."

"I can think of a few other things I've never done before that I'd like to try first," Sam said meaningfully. "Such as doing the wild thing with a certain Southern sweetie who—"

Carrie nudged Sam in the ribs. "Give it a rest, Bridges," she said. "I have a feeling you're more ready to get your palm read than you are to hop into bed with Pres."

"For the moment," Sam said loftily.

Carrie grinned at Sam and rummaged in her purse for some money.

The three best friends, who were all working as au pairs for the summer on Sunset Island, the fabulous, famous resort island off the coast of Maine, were about to spend Sunday afternoon at the Sunset Island Psychic Fair—a biennial event that took place in a cluster of large tents pitched in the main municipal park on the small island.

Carrie had picked Emma and Sam up earlier in her employers' Mercedes. Now, because it was just too cloudy and cool a day to go to the beach, the three of them

3

were about to pass the afternoon at the psychic fair.

As Carrie paid her admission fee she thought once again about the remarkable series of events that had brought her, Emma, and Sam together in the first place. They had met a little over a year before at the International Au Pair Convention in New York City. And even though the three girls were as different from one another as they could possibly be, they had become best friends.

Take Emma, for example, Carrie thought. *An actual heiress! From the Cresswell family of Boston. She's got perfect blond hair and perfect clothes, and she's a French major at Goucher College. Whoever would have thought she'd be one of my best friends? And whoever would have guessed that her life's ambition is to go to Africa and study primates?*

And Sam? Come on! Totally wild, totally outrageous—willing to try anything once. With that hair! And so skinny—not like me. She grew up in Junction, Kansas, with a high-school football coach for a dad and a typical Midwestern mom. She's already been in a Broadway show, and she's the best dancer that I've ever seen.

Who would have thought that Emma and Sam would be friends with me, your basic girl next door from Teaneck, New Jersey, daughter of two doctors and who got good enough grades to get into Yale?

Carrie thought back to how all three of them had gotten hired by different families that summered on amazing Sunset Island. Sometimes she thought that as far as employers went, she was the luckiest of the three girls.

She'd been hired by Graham Perry Templeton—who, as Graham Perry, was the rock and roll legend who had made several multimillion-selling albums and played with the likes of Billy Joel and Neil Young. Carrie took care of Graham and Claudia Templeton's thirteen-year-old son, Ian, and their five-year-old daughter, Chloe.

I can't complain about any of them, Carrie thought. *And the house? It's totally amazing. But no more amazing than the fact that Emma, Sam, and I all have boyfriends we love, and that we're all back on*

5

Sunset Island for the second summer in a row.

Not that there haven't been ups and downs, Carrie recalled. *I mean, Emma's got a huge problem now with—*

"Yo, Carrie, babe," Sam called, tearing Carrie out of her reverie. "Let's get with the program here."

"Yes," Emma joshed, "no trances until you're inside, please."

Carrie laughed and linked arms with her two girlfriends, and the three of them walked into the main tent of the Sunset Island Psychic Fair.

"What a circus!" Sam exclaimed as they made their way through the crowded entrance area. Hundreds of people were milling around the main portion of the first tent, where chairs were lined up by the many booths and tables at which dozens of women and men were giving various kinds of psychic readings.

Carrie could see in the rear lots of different booths where people were selling all kinds of products and books. And along the left side, rows and rows of folding chairs were set up in front of a stage. The sign above the stage read COSMIC MEETING PLACE.

"Seriously New Age," Sam commented.

"Maybe it'll be fun," Emma ventured.

Carrie sighed. *Frankly, I'm skeptical,* she thought. *But on the other hand, maybe there really are some people who are psychic. Look at Darcy, for example!*

Carrie was thinking of their good friend Darcy Laken, who sometimes had flashes about what was going to happen. And she'd been proven right many times.

Maybe I should just ask Darcy what's going to happen with Billy and me, Carrie thought. *Everything is so . . . so up in the air! I love him very much and I'm really glad he's back on the island, but he could leave again any day to go home to Seattle because of his dad, and—*

"Psychic Sam who knows all and tells all says you are thinking about Billy right now," Sam told Carrie.

"Busted," Carrie admitted.

"Everything's going to work out fine," Sam assured Carrie.

"Billy loves you," Emma added.

"I know," Carrie agreed.

"Listen, this place is too cosmic for me." Sam sniffed as a rainbow-suited man with hair tied back in a rainbow-colored headband wandered past them.

"Well, we can each try a different—" Carrie began.

"You!" the rainbow man cried, pointing at Sam.

"Me?"

"You're red," he said.

"Of course," Sam said proudly. She shook her long, curly red hair, and did a little spin to show off the red cropped top under Mickey Mouse suspenders that held up a pair of cutoff jeans. On her feet were her trademark red cowboy boots.

"No," the rainbow man said earnestly. "That's not what I mean at all."

"Well," Carrie said politely to him, "that's interesting. Please excuse us, because—"

"No!" the rainbow man cut her off. "Your friend is red!"

"What are you talking about?" Emma asked him.

Carrie looked around. The whole thing was weird, but she figured they were perfectly safe—there were two uniformed and

8

armed Sunset Island police officers on security duty not more than ten feet away.

"And you," the rainbow man said, pointing to Carrie, "are blue."

"No, I'm not," Carrie replied. "I'm perfectly happy."

"And you're green," he said meaningfully to Emma. "I'm Aura Man," he added by way of explanation.

"I thought you were the rainbow man," Sam said.

Aura Man shook his head. "Uh-uh. Rainbow Man is in booth thirty-four. I'm Aura Man."

"Good to meetcha, Aura babe," Sam said, sticking out her hand for the guy to shake.

He ignored her hand. "You'll find me in booth twenty-three. Rainbow aura readings," he said. "Only ten bucks." He leaned closer to her. "Being red is very significant."

Carrie saw Emma and Sam give him identical looks—looks that said the guy was out of his mind.

"You don't know what you're missing," Aura Man told the three friends. Then he turned on his heel and left.

Five seconds later Carrie heard his voice again, twenty feet away, as he flagged down another visitor to the psychic fair.

"You're orange," Carrie heard him say to a visitor she couldn't see.

"So," Sam told her friends, "now I feel aura-bull." Her friends stared at her as if she was crazy. "Horrible, aura-bull, get it?"

Carrie and Emma groaned loudly at the pun.

"So, which booths should we check out?" Carrie asked them.

Just then the sound of bells came through the loudspeaker system.

"Ladies and gentlemen," a soothing voice announced, "it is now two P.M. The free seminar 'Healing Your Psychic Inner Child' will take place in the Cosmic Meeting Place beginning in five minutes. I repeat, the 'Healing Your Psychic Inner Child' seminar will begin in exactly five minutes."

"Wanna go?" Sam asked dryly.

"I'll pass," Carrie said.

"Me, too," Emma commented.

"My inner child's in great shape," Sam pronounced. "I heal other people's inner children."

"Like you healed Becky and Allie Jacobs," Carrie joked.

Becky and Allie Jacobs were the twin fourteen-year-old girls Sam looked after. She'd been hired by their single dad, Dan Jacobs. Recently Dan had fired Sam because he thought the twins were too old for an au pair. But they'd cleverly coerced their dad into hiring Sam back.

"Unhealable," Sam said. "Beyond help."

"What do you say we split up and look around?" Carrie suggested.

"Good idea," Emma said. "Then we can meet up again in an hour and see if we found anything interesting."

"Cool," Sam commented. "I'm gonna check out guys."

"I'm sure Aura Man is looking for a date," Carrie offered.

"You're blue," Sam joked. "You go out with him."

"So," Emma said, "we'll meet back here in an hour?"

The girls all nodded, and then split up to go in separate directions.

What the heck, Carrie thought, *maybe I'll see someone here I'll want to take pic-*

tures of later in the week. Carrie was an accomplished photographer who had had her photos published in the ultra-hip magazine *Rock On!*

A woman dressed in layers of gauze wafted by, jingling strings of tiny bells wrapped around her wrists. "Peace, love, eternal life," the woman chanted. She smiled at Carrie. "Do you want to know the secret of life?" she asked.

"I think I already know what it is!" Carrie said, a smile playing on her lips. "Don't stop breathing!"

"So," the matronly-looking woman said as Carrie sat down opposite her, "what kind of reading do you want?"

"I'm not sure," Carrie admitted.

"My vibrations are telling me inner child," the woman said, nodding seriously. "My name is Elizabeth, by the way. And yours is . . . ?"

"I thought maybe you could just divine it," Carrie joked.

The psychic didn't smile.

"My name's Carrie Alden," Carrie told her.

"Five dollars for ten minutes," Elizabeth said.

"Okay." Carrie reached into her purse and took out a five-dollar bill, which she handed to the woman.

"It's very hard to do any kind of real work in ten minutes," Elizabeth said, stashing the money in her drawstring purse. "I just want you to know that."

Carrie shrugged. *I'm not about to drop more than five bucks on this thing,* she thought. *I'm only doing it for fun.*

"We'll go to the cards," Elizabeth said. "But first . . ." She lit a stick of incense.

The woman picked up a deck of cards and spread them over the table, facedown.

"Pick one," she said to Carrie.

Carrie flipped one over. It was a card that featured a scene from the old children's TV show *Lassie.*

Elizabeth smiled. "You've got a warm, loving spirit in you," she said.

"Lassie told you that?" Carrie asked.

Elizabeth shot her a look. "Please, if you don't cooperate with the spirits, the spirits won't cooperate with you."

"Sorry," Carrie murmured.

13

"Like a dog," the psychic told her. "Loyal."

Like a dog? Carrie thought skeptically.

"Pick another," Elizabeth instructed Carrie.

Carrie flipped another card. A card with the logo from the TV show *Wheel of Fortune* came up.

"Wait a sec," Carrie said, just as the woman was about to speak. "Is every card in this deck a TV show?"

"Yes," Elizabeth said. She started flipping cards over at random. Carrie saw one that said *Roseanne*, another that read *Baywatch,* and another that read *Mighty Morphin Power Rangers.*

"You're kidding," Carrie said, not sure if this was a joke.

"Kids watch more TV than adults, right?" the psychic asked.

"I guess," Carrie agreed.

"Then your inner child should pick up waves from TV shows," she said triumphantly.

"But—"

"I used to use a regular tarot deck," Elizabeth admitted, "but not enough

14

people could relate to the symbolism. So I had this made."

"Gee," Carrie said, trying to keep a straight face. "It's . . . uh . . . original."

Elizabeth gestured at the cards. "Shuffle again and spread 'em out."

Carrie did as she was told. Then, without waiting for instructions, she picked a card and turned it over.

"*Seinfeld!*" the woman cried. "That's a happy card."

"I've watched the show," Carrie admitted. "It's funny."

"You have a funny inner child," Elizabeth remarked. "Playful, funny—isn't that terrific?"

Carrie looked at her skeptically again. *This whole thing is incredibly stupid,* she thought. *I just wasted five dollars. I can't believe I even wanted to do this.*

"Your time is almost up," the woman warned Carrie. "Unless, of course, you'd like a longer reading . . ."

"Can I ask you a question?" Carrie blurted out, not wanting to leave the table without at least trying to get some insight into her future.

"Sure," said Elizabeth.

"My boyfriend," Carrie asked, her voice hesitating a little. "His father just got out of the hospital. Is he going to be okay?"

The psychic looked at her watch. "Oh, too bad, time's up," she announced.

"But—"

"But what?" the woman said.

"But I asked if I could ask you a question," Carrie said.

"And so you did," Elizabeth replied. "If you want the answer, it's another five dollars for ten more minutes."

Carrie got up from the table. "That is a total rip-off."

"Your vibrations are getting very negative right now," Elizabeth warned.

"If there are any actual psychics in this world, people like you give them a bad name," Carrie fumed. "I asked you a very serious question about something that really concerns me—"

"What do you do for a living?" the woman interrupted.

"What does that have to do with anything?" Carrie asked with exasperation.

"Just tell me," the psychic said.

16

"I'm an au pair," Carrie replied.

"Okay, you're a baby-sitter," Elizabeth translated. "So if you were baby-sitting for my kids and I was paying you five dollars an hour, and then I asked you to stay more than an hour, wouldn't you expect to get paid for it?"

"It's not the same," Carrie fumed. "Just forget the whole thing."

"Wait, I'll give you a final bit of free advice," Elizabeth said, "since I don't want you to leave here with so much negative energy."

"So what's the advice?" Carrie asked warily, her hands on her hips.

"Watch more TV," Elizabeth counseled her. "Remember, the answers are all in the shows."

TWO

"You want another slice of pizza?" Billy asked Carrie.

"I already ate two," she said ruefully, patting her stomach.

"So?" Billy asked, reaching for another slice. "As far as I'm concerned, two slices of pizza are barely an appetizer."

It was the next day, and Carrie had managed to sneak in a few afternoon hours off while the Templeton kids, Ian and Chloe, went to Portland with their mom. She and Billy had bought a pizza at a new place on the boardwalk. Now they were sitting on the beach, eating pizza and drinking cherry slushes.

Carrie looked down at the new bathing suit she'd bought at the Cheap Boutique,

19

everyone's favorite hip clothing store on the island. It was a two-piece suit—something she usually stayed away from because she thought her hips were too big—in blue and white polka dots. The legs were boy-cut, and the top wasn't too skimpy. *It's not exactly a teeny-weeny bikini like Sam wears,* Carrie thought, *but it's pretty daring for me.*

"If I ate as much as you eat, I'd look like the Goodyear blimp," Carrie told Billy, brushing some crumbs off her legs.

Billy grinned. "Yeah, but you'd be *my* blimp."

Carrie swatted Billy's leg. "Thanks a lot!"

He leaned over and gave her a kiss. "Carrie, you're gorgeous, you're perfect, and I'm crazy about you. Is that better?"

"Much," Carrie said with a laugh.

She thought for maybe the zillionth time how much she loved Billy. *I am so lucky,* she thought. *He's such a terrific guy—smart, sensitive, talented, kind, sweet, gorgeous, and mine. And I was so lonely when he went home because of his dad's accident.*

I don't know what I'd do if he went back to Seattle permanently.

". . . so Pres and I are almost through with this new demo tape," Billy was saying.

"What?" Carrie asked, sipping on her cherry slush. "I was lost in thought."

"I said we're doing a demo of four tunes Pres and I wrote," Billy repeated. "I really think this might finally persuade Polimar Records to sign us."

"They signed you guys once before," Carrie reminded him.

"Well, Diana ruined that," Billy said, finishing his slice of pizza and reaching for a napkin. "And Diana is no longer in the Flirts, so that is ancient history."

"Sam and Emma didn't mention you were doing a new demo," Carrie said.

"We're not using the backup singers on this tape," Billy explained. "It's real basic. I hate to get my hopes up, but . . ."

Carrie touched his cheek. "But your hopes are up."

"I admit it," Billy said. He leaned back on his elbows and lifted his face to the warm afternoon sun. "Mmmm, this feels great."

"It does," Carrie agreed. She stretched out next to him. "Did you miss this when you were in Seattle?"

"It's never sunny in Seattle," he said with a laugh. He turned to Carrie. "Actually, what I missed was you."

"I know," she said quietly.

"It was horrible, Car, I mean it," Billy said. He rolled over and put his arms around her. "I never want to go through that again."

"I second that," Carrie murmured.

"It was . . . it was kind of hard, you know?" Billy went on earnestly. "I mean, explaining what I do here to my family."

"You're a talented, successful musician with his own band," Carrie said. "What is there to explain?"

Billy sighed and put his arms under his head. "If I'm so talented and successful, how come I don't have a recording contract, for one thing?"

"Well, because it takes time—"

"I know that," Billy interrupted. "But try telling my mom."

"You have to live your own life," Carrie said firmly.

"I know that too, babe," Billy said. "And music is all I care about—other than you, that is. I just wish my family understood."

They were quiet for a few minutes. Carrie looked around her. In the distance the waves crashed into the shore. A pretty girl in a white bikini threw a Frisbee to her German shepherd, who caught it in his teeth and raced back to her.

Everything is so perfect here, she thought. *But back in Seattle Billy's dad is still struggling to regain his strength, and Billy's family doesn't understand what his life is all about.*

"Do they expect you to go back to Seattle?" Carrie finally asked in a low voice. *Please let him say no,* Carrie thought fiercely.

"No," Billy said.

Carrie let go of the deep breath she hadn't even realized she was holding.

"They wouldn't do that," Billy said. "I mean, they might think it—"

"But they wouldn't say it," Carrie finished for him.

23

"Right," Billy said. He turned back to Carrie and brushed a strand of hair off her face. "Sometimes I have this wild fantasy. . . ."

"What?" Carrie asked softly.

"That you and I move to Seattle together," Billy said. "We get a little house, I help take care of Dad's business. . . ."

"And what do I do, play house?" Carrie asked, sounding harsher than she'd intended.

"You go to college in Seattle," Billy said. "And you roam around the city taking these incredible photos."

"And what happens to the Flirts in this fantasy?" Carrie asked. "Does the whole band move to Seattle, too?"

Billy smiled. "Why not? After all, it's my fantasy. I can run it any way I want."

"Well, right now I'd like to fantasize about a swim and turn it into reality," Carrie said, jumping up.

"Hey, I freaked you out just now, didn't I?" Billy said, touching Carrie's arm.

"No," Carrie assured him.

"Yes, I did," Billy said. He put his arms around her. "Don't worry, Car, it's not reality. I'm staying right here. Everything is cool."

But even as Carrie lifted her lips for his kiss, she wondered if everything was really so cool after all.

"So the way I see it," Ian was telling Carrie as they walked along the boardwalk that evening, "is that there's going to be a serious music revolution. Rap is over. Heavy metal is so totally five minutes ago. Industrial music is going to be the next thing!"

Carrie tried to look interested, but her mind was still on what Billy had told her on the beach that afternoon. *How can he be having a fantasy about me stuck in some little house in Seattle?* she thought anxiously. *That's more my idea of a nightmare!*

Carrie, Ian, and little Chloe were walking down the boardwalk on their way to the Golden Dragon, a Chinese restaurant. Claudia had come home from Portland with a splitting headache and asked Carrie to take the kids out to dinner so she could lie down.

"Can I get fortune cookies?" Chloe asked, skipping along beside Carrie.

"Sure," Carrie said.

"So, what do you think?" Ian asked.

"About what?" Carrie replied.

"About the music revolution that we were just talking about," Ian said with exasperation.

"Oh, that," Carrie said.

Ian gave her an arch look. "Why do I have this feeling you aren't listening to me, Carrie?"

"I am," Carrie insisted as she opened the door to the restaurant.

"No, you're not," Ian said. "I might be thirteen and a half, but I'm not stupid."

"I'm sorry," said Carrie with a sigh. "I just have something on my mind."

"Billy?" Chloe asked, then she giggled and clapped her hand over her mouth.

"Well, you're pretty smart for a five-year-old!" Carrie exclaimed, bending down to tickle the little girl in the ribs.

"How many?" a pretty Asian girl asked them.

"Three, please," Carrie told her.

"There will be about a ten-minute wait for a table," the girl told Carrie.

"Okay, we'll wait. The name is Alden."

Carrie and Ian sat on a small red bench. Chloe jumped into Carrie's lap. "I'm hungry now," Chloe said.

"You'll only have to wait a few minutes," Carrie assured her.

"Listen, about relationships," Ian began. "Take it from me. They're not worth it."

Carrie bit her lip so she wouldn't smile. "And since when did you get so worldly?" she asked him.

"Since I was stupid enough to fall for Becky Jacobs," Ian replied. "Bad move. I should have been concentrating on my music, but I got distracted by a babe."

"Uh-huh," Carrie said. She knew that Becky had broken up with him. *I guess love is hard at any age.*

"I wanted you to look at some new lyrics I wrote," Ian told Carrie. He reached into his back pocket and pulled out a folded sheet of paper. "I mean, if you want to, that is," he added shyly.

"I'd love to," Carrie told him, smiling at the boy. *He's really such a sweetheart,* she thought. *It's just that it's hard for him to live in the shadow of his famous father. Sometimes he doesn't know how to handle it.*

"Don't look at that now," Chloe pouted. "I'm hungry!"

"We have to wait for a table," Ian reminded her, "so chill."

"I don't want to chill, I'm hungry!" Chloe whined.

"Quit being such a brat!" Ian yelled at her.

"I'm not a brat!" Chloe yelled back, her lower lip starting to tremble.

"I'll get you some crunchy noodles," Carrie told the little girl. "Okay?"

Chloe nodded, her eyes full of tears. Carrie hurried over to the hostess and asked her for some noodles for a starving five-year-old. Carrie brought the bowl over to Chloe, who immediately began munching.

"You shouldn't just give in to her when she's a brat, you know," Ian said. "She only does it for attention."

"I do not," Chloe said between mouthfuls.

She stuck out her tongue, covered with half-chewed noodle bits, at her brother.

"Get a life," Ian muttered.

Chloe grinned triumphantly.

I wish I were anyplace but here right now, Carrie said to herself. *The next thing you know, the two of them will be having a food fight. I wish I were with Billy and he was telling me that the whole fantasy he came up with this afternoon was a figment of my imagination.*

"So, these are my new lyrics," Ian said diffidently, handing Carrie the sheet of paper.

"It's probably not good," Chloe said gleefully.

"Shut up!" yelled Ian.

"You shut up!" Chloe screamed.

"Both of you cut it out," Carrie said sharply. She took a deep breath. "Come on, you guys. You don't usually act like this." She turned to Chloe. "I want you to be quiet now and let me read Ian's new song."

"Okay," Chloe decided.

"I call it 'Just That Kind of Girl,'" Ian said nervously, biting a fingernail. "It's kind of about Becky. It's not done yet."

So what if she says she loves you
It's just some stupid words
So what if she says she wants you
It's just some stuff she's heard
So what if you feel like dying
And there isn't any cure
She doesn't care, she'll leave you there
She's just that kind of girl

"I know, it stinks!" Ian said, reaching for the lyric sheet.

"It doesn't stink," Carrie insisted. She was in a state of shock. She had never seen Ian display any real talent as a lyricist. *But this is really good,* she thought.

"It doesn't stink?" Ian echoed hopefully.

"Ian, this is terrific!" Carrie exclaimed. "I'm . . . I'm totally impressed!"

"Really?" Ian asked.

"Really! You're very talented!"

"Oh, yeah, I know," Ian said, trying hard to sound tough and nonchalant. "I mean, other people might have doubted me, but I never doubted myself."

"You should write some real music to this," Carrie said, "not just the kind of stuff the Zits do."

"But that would be turning my back on industrial music!" Ian protested. "I can't do that!"

"Carrie, I ate all the noodles and I'm still hungry," Chloe said. She showed Carrie the empty wooden bowl.

"I'm sure we'll be seated in a minute," Carrie told the little girl. She turned back to Ian. "Listen, Ian, this song is really good. It's the best thing you've ever written, and—"

"Hi there!" came a familiar female voice.

Carrie looked up. There was Darcy Laken, dressed in jeans and a University of Maine sweatshirt. Her gorgeous long black hair was up in a ponytail.

"Hi," Carrie said. "I haven't seen you in days."

"Between summer school and everything else, I've been really busy," Darcy said. "Hi, kids," she added.

"How's Molly doing?" Ian asked.

He was referring to Molly Mason, Darcy's sixteen-year-old friend. Molly had been in a terrible car accident and was a paraplegic confined to a wheelchair. Darcy lived with Molly and her parents and helped to take

31

care of Molly. Since Darcy and Molly were best friends and Molly's horror-movie-writing parents were paying Darcy's college tuition, the arrangement was working out well for everyone.

"She's pretty good," Darcy said. "Let me just see if our order is ready—I already called it in."

Darcy went over to talk to the hostess, then she came back. "Another ten minutes," she reported. "This place is always so backed up, but they have the best Chinese food on the island." She leaned against the wall and folded her arms. "So, how's life?"

"Okay," Carrie said. "We thought about you yesterday—we went to the psychic fair."

Darcy laughed. "Why waste your money?"

"How can you say that when you're psychic yourself?" Carrie wondered.

Darcy shrugged. "I don't know. I guess the whole thing just makes me uncomfortable. I think there are a lot of crooks at those psychic fair things. Why, did you solve all the mysteries of the universe?"

"No," Carrie admitted. "In fact, I got taken big-time."

"Big-time?" Darcy echoed.

"Well, over five dollars' worth," Carrie told her with a laugh. "But in my humble opinion Chloe is more psychic than this woman was."

"What's psychic?" Chloe asked.

"Someone who can, like, tell the future," Ian explained. He cocked his head at Darcy. "So, just how psychic are you, exactly?"

"Oh, not so much," Darcy muttered.

It's amazing that it makes her so uncomfortable, Carrie thought. *If I had a talent like hers, I'd be proud of it.*

"You mean you can really see into the future?" Ian wondered.

"Well, every once in a while," Darcy said. "But I never know when it's going to happen—when I'm going to know something about the future. And sometimes I can't even tell I'm getting a message about something. It's kind of weird."

I wish I could ask her what's going to happen with me and Billy, Carrie thought. *It would be so wonderful if I didn't have to wonder and worry about it.*

33

But then a terrible thought occurred to her. *What if I asked Darcy and she really did know, and what she told me was not something that I want to hear? Would I want to know then?* Carrie wondered. *Would I?*

"I was wondering," Carrie began slowly.

"Hmmm?" Darcy asked, checking out the sports highlights being shown on the TV in the bar area.

"Do you ever . . . I mean, have you ever had any of your psychic flashes about . . . oh, say, me and Billy?"

"That guy was totally safe at third," Darcy groused. She tore her eyes away from the TV. "What did you say?"

"Miss, your take-out order is ready," the hostess called to Darcy.

"Oh, thanks," Darcy said.

"And your table is ready. Sorry for the wait," she added to Carrie.

"I'm not hungry anymore!" Chloe complained.

"So, I'll see you soon," Darcy said. "Say hi to Sam and Emma from me and Molly, okay?"

"Sure," Carrie said, ushering Ian and Chloe ahead of her.

It was probably stupid of me to ask Darcy that question anyway, Carrie thought with chagrin. *I'm not even sure I believe Darcy really has ESP. Still, I wonder what she would have said. . . .*

And I wonder if I could live with it, whatever it was.

THREE

"It was amazing, Carrie!" Emma exclaimed.

"I can't believe this," Carrie replied. "You were so skeptical."

"I was," Emma agreed, "but not so much anymore."

It was the next afternoon. Emma had brought Katie, one of the three Hewitt children in her charge, to the Templetons' for a play date with Chloe. Emma and Carrie were hanging out near the huge backyard pool in their swimsuits, while Katie and Chloe played on the jungle gym. Ian was up in his room, finishing the lyrics to "That Kind of Girl."

Emma was filling Carrie in on the psychic reading she'd gotten on Sunday. Earlier she had explained to Carrie that she'd been reluctant to tell her and Sam because it sounded so strange, but when Carrie mentioned to her what she'd wanted to ask Darcy, Emma had changed her mind about telling her.

"Her name is Mrs. Ricci," Emma began, "and she started me out with a basic astrological reading."

Carrie resettled her sunglasses on her nose. "And?" she said.

"Everything she said was exactly right!" Emma cried. "I told her my birthday— February eleventh—and where I was born, and what time, and then she looked in some sort of book and told me the most amazing things!"

"For example?" Carrie asked her, still not sure that any of this made sense.

"Well," Emma said, sitting up, "she said I was friendly to everyone, but consider only a select few to be my true friends."

"That's true," Carrie said thoughtfully. "Me, and Sam, and Diana De Witt."

Emma laughed, because Carrie had just added to the list the name of their arch-enemy on the island. Along with her friend

Lorell Courtland, Diana seemed to have no goal in life other than to make Emma, Carrie, and Sam as miserable as possible. And she was good at it.

"I'd leave Diana out if I was counting buddies," Emma commented dryly.

"So what else did this Mrs. Ricci say?" Carrie asked.

"She said that like a lot of Aquarians, I'm a little quirky—"

"That's true," Carrie put in. "For instance, ninety percent of the time you dress in white."

"—and that my approach to life is to care about ideas and causes," Emma continued.

"Okay, that's true," Carrie agreed. "You do care about COPE."

COPE, which was the acronym for Citizens of Positive Ethics, was a local organization on Sunset Island that advocated protection of the island's fragile ecosystem, as well as help for the poorer year-round island residents.

"Right," Emma agreed. "Don't you think that's amazing?"

"Not really," Carrie replied. "I mean, the

things she said were general enough to apply to just about anyone, don't you think?"

"There's more," Emma said. "She said—don't laugh—that men find me fascinating."

"Of course she did," Carrie said. "What girl wouldn't want to hear that?"

Emma laughed. "Well, I'm not saying it's necessarily true."

"In your case it is true, though," Carrie acknowledged grudgingly.

"She told me so much," Emma said, sitting up and hugging her knees to her chest. "She said I've had more adventures than most girls my age—"

"Also true," Carrie commented. "You've traveled all over the world. Maybe it was a lucky guess."

"But this is the most incredible part. It was about perfume!"

"Perfume?"

Emma nodded.

"Aha!" Carrie cried. "She wanted to sell you perfume! I knew it all the time!"

"No," Emma said, "she didn't have anything to sell. She just wanted to do what was best for my inner being."

"Your inner being?" Carrie repeated.

Emma reached for the sunblock and poured some on her legs. "Anyway, Mrs. Ricci said that my inner being would do best with clean, fresh-smelling scents."

"Sunset Magic!" Carrie exclaimed.

"Exactly!" Emma agreed.

Sunset Magic was the perfume that Emma and Carrie had jointly developed, with the help of their friend Erin Kane's father, who was a professional "nose," or perfume creator. The two girls and Mr. Kane had manufactured a batch of Sunset Magic, and it was already being sold on the island in places such as the Cheap Boutique, where Erin worked.

"Hey, maybe you should have tried to sell our perfume to her!" Carrie said with a laugh. "Let me use that sunblock when you're done, okay?"

"Listen to this," Emma said, handing the bottle to Carrie. "She said that she saw me being involved with perfume in some way, that scent was going to change my destiny."

"Meaning that we're going to make a fortune from our perfume?" Carrie asked.

"I don't know," Emma admitted. "But she said that bad energy had created a hostile environment within my family, and that there had been major changes."

"Like your mother cutting you off without a penny," Carrie pointed out.

"Right," Emma agreed. "And Mrs. Ricci said perfume would change all that."

Carrie finished rubbing the sunblock into her legs. "She really said all that?"

"She did," Emma confirmed. "Now, you can't tell me that all that is so general she could have said it about anyone, can you?"

"No, I really can't," Carrie said thoughtfully. "What did you say her name was again?"

"Mrs. Ricci," Emma repeated. "She looked so normal and ordinary, Carrie. I never thought I'd believe in any of this. I did it for fun, just like you and Sam did."

"How much did she charge you?" Carrie inquired.

"Five dollars," Emma said, "which is just about all I can afford these days. It was only supposed to be a ten-minute reading, but she ended up spending twenty minutes with me at least, and she didn't charge me another penny extra."

"A psychic with a heart," Carrie murmured.

"There's more," Emma said, leaning close to Carrie.

"What?" Carrie asked. She reached for her apple juice and took a long swallow.

"Well, she asked me to give her something that had been mine for a very long time."

"Like what?" Carrie asked, not understanding. "To keep?"

"No," Emma replied. "To get a deeper reading. I gave her the little silver ring I always wear, the one my father gave me."

"What did she do with it?" Carrie queried.

"She held it in her hand," Emma said. "So as to get my vibrations, she said."

"Yeah, right," Carrie scoffed.

"Wait, don't judge, just listen," Emma said, holding her hand up.

"So then what?" Carrie prompted.

"She asked me to ask her some questions," Emma said.

"Did you?"

"I asked her about my mother," Emma said. "And get this: she told me *exactly* what the trouble was."

"How?" Carrie asked her.

"She said I was having problems with my mother, and it might seem as if it was about money," Emma explained, "but what it really is about is power."

"Wow," Carrie said, genuinely impressed.

Just then the phone rang, and Carrie got up to get it. But by the time she picked it up, she could hear that Ian had already gotten it on the upstairs phone, so she hung up immediately.

Carrie put the phone down and turned back to Emma. "That *is* pretty amazing, what she said about your mother."

"She also told me that my father couldn't help me, because he had problems of his own," Emma said.

"Okay, now I'm getting weirded out," Carrie said. "How could she know that your dad lost his fortune in the stock market and your mom disinherited you?"

"That's exactly what I wondered," Emma agreed.

44

"So what else did she say?" Carrie asked, fascinated now in spite of herself.

"She said I should just do my best," Emma explained, "and work on my own projects."

"Sunset Magic!" Carrie cried.

"I think so," Emma agreed. "I think that's what she was talking about."

"Amazing," Carrie murmured. She lay back on the chaise lounge and closed her eyes. *Maybe I should go see this Mrs. Ricci,* she thought. *Maybe it's not entirely crazy. I could certainly use some good advice about Billy. . . .*

"Maybe you should go talk with her," Emma gently suggested.

Carrie laughed. "Watch out, Em, you just read my mind!"

"The psychic fair is going on all week," Emma continued. "It's not expensive, and it certainly couldn't hurt. I know you feel confused about what to do if Billy has to go back to Seattle—"

"Oh, God, I hate to think about it," Carrie moaned.

"I know," Emma commiserated. "And

maybe this psychic thing really is stupid. But even if all it does is help you sort out your own feelings, it'll be worth it, don't you think?"

"I don't know what to think anymore," Carrie replied. She turned slightly and leaned on one elbow. "You know what Billy told me? He said that—"

Just then Ian Templeton came running out through the sliding glass doors, yelling at the top of his lungs.

"We did it!" he screamed. "We did it, we did it, we did it, we did it, *we did it!*"

Then he ran toward the pool, took a tremendous bounce on the diving board, and—still dressed in his shorts, T-shirt, and sneakers—did a cannonball dive, splashing Carrie and Emma.

"I think Ian has finally lost his mind," Carrie said, wiping the water from her face.

"He really did just jump in there with all his clothes on, right?" Emma asked.

"Right," Carrie replied. She stood up and walked to the edge of the pool, where Ian had just surfaced. Katie and Chloe ran over from the jungle gym.

"Ian went in the pool with his regular clothes on!" Chloe exclaimed.

"So I see," Carrie agreed, putting her arm around the little girl.

Emma padded over to the edge of the pool and looked down.

"We did it!" Ian sputtered as he held on to the edge of the pool. "This is the greatest day of my life!"

"Can I help you out of the pool?" Carrie asked him politely.

Ian nodded, and Carrie and Emma reached down, each of them taking one of Ian's hands. But Ian pulled hard, and, caught off balance, the two of them fell into the pool with him.

"Hey, you pulled them in!" Katie cried, jumping up and down.

"Everyone should be in here!" Ian yelled back to the little girl. "Come on, you guys! We need to celebrate!"

"What is going on?" Carrie gasped when she surfaced, water streaming off her face. "What are you *doing*, Ian?"

"I wasn't planning on a swim, Ian," Emma said, treading water.

"We're coming in, too!" Chloe yelled. She and Katie went around to the shallow end and climbed in.

"Now that we're all soaking wet, do you want to tell us what this is all about?" Carrie asked Ian.

"We did it," Ian said again, proudly.

"I'm a little lost here," Carrie said as she, Emma, and Ian swam over to the shallow end. "And I don't think this is funny."

"Remember the movie *Sunset Beach Slaughter?*" Ian said. He was so excited he could barely get the words out of his mouth.

"Yes," Carrie said. *Of course I remember it! I was in it! And I made five thousand dollars for playing the slasher's first victim. Molly Mason's mother and father were the screenwriters. I almost lost my au pair job because I got so involved with that project.*

"Remember the song I wrote for it? The one the Zits recorded?" Ian continued eagerly.

He began to sing—chant, actually, at the top of his lungs.

48

He came in the night
His face was such a fright.
And when the deed was over,
He was feeling quite all right!

He really felt the pressure,
It took him by the hand.
He really tried to fight it,
He didn't understand.

And finally it beat him,
It undermined his life.
He felt the only answer was
To kill 'em with a knife!

When Ian was done, he took the forefinger of his right hand and drew it sharply across his throat, as if slashing himself to death.

"A lovely tune," Emma teased, floating on her back a moment. "So poetic."

What's this all about? Carrie wondered. "I remember," she said to Ian. "Duke Underwood was supposed to give the tape to the head of Westwood Studios, right?"

Duke Underwood was the star of the hit TV show *Hollywood High,* and he was also the male star of *Sunset Beach Slaughter.*

Ian couldn't contain himself anymore. "My song's in the movie!" he yelled. "The Zits got their song in the movie!"

"You're kidding," Emma said, nearly dumbfounded.

"Am not!" Ian yelled. "I just got a call from Tommy Shih-Goldman, the head of publicity at Westwood Studios. He said they'd picked us to be on the soundtrack. He asked me to send him my bio!"

"That's incredible," Carrie said.

If Tommy Shih-Goldman called him, it must be true, Carrie thought. *He's the guy who confirmed for me that I could take photographs on the set of the movie when it was being shot here.*

"What's a bio?" Ian asked.

"It's the story of your life," Carrie explained. "A biography."

"Oh," Ian said, his face brightening. "Anyway, you know what's cool?"

"What?" Emma asked him.

"The Zits are gonna be the first Sunset

Island band to have a song on a movie soundtrack! We're gonna be bigger than the Flirts!"

Carrie frowned. "Did Tommy Shih-Goldman say how many of your dad's songs are on the soundtrack?" she asked.

"Oh, a couple, I think," Ian said breezily. "But that's not why they picked my song—the Zits made it on talent."

Somehow I doubt that, Carrie thought. *They probably used Ian's song to get some from his famous father, but I'm not about to burst Ian's bubble by telling him that.*

"I'm telling you, we're on our way!" Ian yelled, splashing around in the water. "This is only the beginning! I knew it would happen! I just knew it!"

Maybe Ian ought to consult with Mrs. Ricci, too, Carrie thought. *He might be able to get the lowdown on what his future is going to be! And whether everyone is bending over backward for him because his dad just happens to be Graham Perry.*

"That's great, Ian," Emma said warmly. "I'm proud of you."

"Yeah," Ian said. "It's cool. And you want to know what's gonna be even cooler?"

"What?" Carrie asked.

"When I kick Becky out of the band," Ian replied. "I can't wait to see the look on her face!"

FOUR

"I didn't think Pres could cook," Carrie said dubiously as she pressed the doorbell of the Flirts's house.

"Me neither," Sam admitted. "Hey, can you believe I actually used to live here?" she asked her friend.

"For about a day," Carrie said with a laugh.

When Dan Jacobs had decided to fire Sam—temporarily, as it turned out—she had gone through total hell trying to find a new job and a new place to live. She had spent several days sleeping on the couch in the Flirts's house—until she flooded the house and Billy and Pres asked her to leave. It had all turned out okay, though. The twins had gone on a hunger strike to ensure Sam's return. And Sam had even managed to get a raise and some other terrific concessions from the Jacobs family, just because they were so desperate to get her back!

"Maybe they're ordering in pizza," Sam said, ringing the doorbell again.

"Nope," Carrie said. "Billy specifically said that Pres was going to do the cooking. Did he ever cook for you?"

"No," Sam declared. "Never. He did put together a couple of romantic picnics, though. Yum!"

"Down, girl," Carrie said with a laugh. She pressed the doorbell again. "I wonder why no one's answering."

Earlier in the day Pres and Billy had called and invited Carrie and Sam on a dinner double date. And then, about an hour later, they'd called back and changed the location of the dinner from a restaurant in Portland to the Flirts's own house.

"Billy never cooked for me, either," Carrie said. "Do you think we should have stopped at McDonald's?"

"I'm glad you brought cheese and crackers," Sam said. "At least we won't go completely hungry."

"I don't know what's keeping them," Carrie said, pressing the doorbell again insistently. "The doorbell works, doesn't it? I can't hear it ring."

"Yeah, it works," Sam said. "You can hear it inside."

"It's probably one of the few things you didn't break when you lived here," Carrie teased.

"Oh, very funny," Sam said. She looked down at herself. "We definitely look too hot to be left out here all alone!"

Both Sam and Carrie had dressed up for the dinner just as if they were going to a fancy restaurant. In fact, Billy had asked that they wear something special—he said that he and Pres were going to do the same, just for fun.

Sam had on one of her Samstyles—the original outfits she designed from draped fabric, secondhand clothing, and vintage pins that were sold at the Cheap Boutique. This one featured an antique, lacy, pale pink bed jacket over a low-cut white cotton slip covered with black velvet hearts. Sam had created a matching black velvet hat with a flower that sat right over her forehead, her wild red hair streaming down her back. And Carrie, who never really felt comfortable putting on fancy clothes, had gone through her closet about a million times before settling on a plain black minidress with a flared skirt, over which she wore an embroidered vest in rust, gold, and black.

"*You're* too hot, maybe," Carrie commented.

"Gimme a break, Jersey girl," Sam sniffed. "If I had hooters like yours, I'd be showing them off, not covering them up."

"Did I ever mention that you are breast-obsessed?" Carrie asked.

"America is breast-obsessed," Sam replied loftily. "I am merely a reflection of my messed-up culture. And besides, if I had hooters, I could rule the world."

Just then the door swung open.

"Did I hear the magic word *hooters?*" Billy said, a broad smile on his face.

He was dressed in a black tuxedo, with a bow tie, starched white shirt, and paisley

vest. He even had a fresh rosebud in his lapel.

"Wow, you look great," Carrie murmured, surprised and pleased.

"You, too," Billy said appreciatively. He reached forward and gave Carrie a warm hug.

"I didn't even know you owned a tuxedo," Carrie marveled.

"Ah, there is much you do not know," Billy said mysteriously.

"Don't forget me," Sam reminded him. "Anyone who looks as good as you should be hugging me, too."

Billy grinned and gave Sam a friendly hug.

"Okay," Sam ordered. "Enough. I want to see the man from Tennessee." She pushed her way past Billy and Carrie in mock haste. They followed her into the living room.

"What have you done in here?" Carrie asked in amazement when she saw the room.

"Just a little redecorating," Billy quipped. The room was entirely lit by candles.

There were about two dozen of them burning in various sizes and shapes of candleholders. Fresh flowers filled three vases. Sandalwood incense burned in a small holder near the table.

"Wow," Carrie said, still amazed. "Want to come redo my room?"

"Hey, can I move back in?" Sam asked innocently. "Looks like my kind of place."

For a split second Billy had a look of total dismay on his face.

"Gee, can't you take a joke?" Sam laughed, and Billy laughed with her.

"You move in," Billy joked, "I move out. What do you say, Carrie? We'll find a place just the two of us—as far away from Hurricane Sam as possible."

I'll consider it, Carrie thought. *As long as it isn't a small cottage in Seattle!*

"Cool," Sam said. "That leaves me with Pres."

"Did someone call my name?" drawled a familiar voice.

Like Billy, Pres had dressed in a black tuxedo for dinner. But instead of a black bow tie, he had on a bolo tie with what looked like a chunk of amber at the neck, and instead of the usual black patent leather shoes that go with a tuxedo, he wore gorgeous gold snakeskin cowboy boots that Carrie knew he wore only on very special occasions.

"Wow," Carrie said as she watched Sam embrace her boyfriend. "Nice tux, Pres."

"Double wow," Sam echoed, letting go and giving Pres a good look from top to bottom. "Dang, boy," she drawled, imitating him, "you look good enough to eat, little darlin'."

Pres laughed and wrapped his arms around Sam's waist. "I don't sound a thing like that."

"Wanna bet?" Sam asked. "But I forgive you because you look so fine tonight."

"You're all heart," Pres said, giving Sam another hug.

"You guys both look so incredible," Carrie said. "And the house . . ."

"They must want something," Sam decided. She put her hands on her hips. "Okay, spit it out. What's the scam?"

Pres shook his head regretfully. "She has no faith in us, Billy."

"I for one am cut to the quick," Billy

agreed solemnly. He turned to Pres. "What is 'the quick,' by the way?"

"I have no idea," Pres admitted. "But I'm cut to it, too."

"I've got a great idea," Sam said.

"What?" Billy asked her.

"Don't cook, don't move, don't even breathe," Sam said. "Just stand there so we can look at you."

Pres winked at her. "Excuse me," he said, "but the kitchen calls." He turned back to the kitchen, from which wonderful smells were wafting.

"So," Billy said, reaching for a bottle that was chilling in an ice bucket on the living room table, "champagne, anyone?"

"*Champagne?*" Carrie echoed.

"Good champagne," Billy specified.

"But you guys can't afford champagne!" Carrie exclaimed.

"Carrie, shut up," Sam said. "I love champagne."

"But—" Carrie began.

"But nothing," Sam said. "Whatever is going on, I like it."

"But—" Carrie tried again.

"Your problem, Car," Sam said, "is that

you lack an adventuresome spirit." She turned to Billy. "Pop the bubbly, big guy."

Billy quickly poured three glasses, handed one each to Sam and Carrie, and held his own up high.

"Here's to the two finest women in the room," he proposed.

"You meant to say 'in the world,' right?" Sam asked.

"Absolutely," Billy agreed, and they all clinked their glasses together and sipped their champagne.

"I'm serious, Billy," Carrie said, taking a seat on the couch. "Where'd you guys get the tuxedos?"

"It's a secret," Billy replied, sitting down next to her. He gazed at her face. "You look really beautiful in candlelight, Car."

She smiled lovingly at him. "So do you," she said softly.

"So do I, but Pres is in the kitchen, so if the two of you start kissing I'm gonna be really ticked off," Sam said as she seated herself in an overstuffed chair.

Billy sat back and took another sip of champagne. "About the tuxes—a buddy of

Jake's works at the tux shop on Main Street. He lent 'em to us for the night."

"Don't ever change," Carrie said softly.

"I have a feeling you're not talking about the tux," Billy replied in a low voice.

"You're right," Carrie admitted. "I want everything to stay just the way it is right now."

"I won't change," Billy said, leaning over to kiss her softly. "I promise."

"Yum," Carrie said, patting her stomach.

"Sensational," Sam echoed.

"Good?" Pres asked.

"Better than that," Sam said. "You're hired."

"Y'all had better save room for dessert," Pres warned, and everybody groaned.

They were sitting around the table in the dining room, which, like the living room, had been utterly transformed by Pres and Billy for the evening meal.

The lights had all been dimmed, the table was covered with an immaculate white tablecloth, and instead of the usual rock and roll music that filled the house, the radio was playing soft jazz from the

National Public Radio station in Portland.

What a feast, Carrie thought as she looked over the remains of their dinner. *Shrimp cocktail. Lobster tails with asparagus. Linguini on the side. A fresh fruit platter. And now this!*

Pres brought in on a platter four tall ice cream parfaits, each covered with fresh whipped cream and topped with a cherry. He put them on the table with a flourish.

"Okay," Carrie said weakly, "I give in." She picked up her spoon and took a bite.

"Eat up," Billy said with a mischievous twinkle in his eye. "Because we're going on the road in fourteen days."

Sam and Carrie both looked up from their dessert in surprise. Billy and Pres had been talking about a short in-state tour for the Flirts, but this was the first time that they'd even mentioned a date.

"No way," Sam said.

"Yes way," Pres drawled. "We made the final arrangements with Polimar Records this afternoon. It's a go."

"And you're the photographer," Billy said, smiling at Carrie.

"That's fantastic!" Carrie gasped.

63

"Omigod!" Sam screamed. "That's what this is all about! How did you guys keep it a secret during the entire meal?"

"We're tough," Billy said with a grin.

Sam leapt up and threw her arms about Pres's neck. "I am so psyched!"

"You've got work," Carrie cautioned.

"Hey, after the way Dan Jacobs begged me to take my job back, I can wrap him around my little finger," Sam bragged. "No prob!"

"Well, it's a prob for me," Carrie said with a sigh. "*I've* got work."

"We'll figure something out," Sam said.

"Like what?" Carrie asked. "Claudia isn't going to give me time off!"

"But when you tell Graham it's for a tour, won't he say okay?" Sam asked.

"I don't know," Carrie said. "But I'll be miserable if you all get to go and I don't!"

As they ate, Billy talked about the plan they had worked out with Polimar Records. The Flirts were going to do four consecutive nights of gigs, starting in Bangor, then Waterville, then Lewiston, and ending in Portland. A Polimar A&R exec would be traveling with them.

"And here's the best part," Billy said. "If he's happy, we get the recording deal."

"I'm gonna do my damnedest to make him happy," Pres drawled, his voice deadly serious for once.

"We will, my man," Billy said with conviction. "This is our time. I can feel it."

They've come so close to a deal with Polimar so many times, Carrie thought, looking at Billy's hopeful face. *And they deserve it so much. . . .*

"It'll be so much more fun being on tour with Erin than it was when Diana was in the band," Sam said. In addition to having a fabulous singing voice, Erin was also really cool and nice. Everyone liked her as much as they disliked Diana.

Carrie got a faraway look in her eyes. "I wish Sly could be there," she said quietly.

The whole room grew quiet. Carrie was talking about Sly Smith, the longtime drummer for the Flirts, who had developed full-blown AIDS earlier in the summer and had to leave the island to seek treatment at John Hopkins Medical Center in his hometown, Baltimore.

He's out of the hospital now, Carrie recalled, *but he's still really sick and that picture he sent of himself was so awful! I wanted to cry when Billy showed it to me.*

"The best thing we can do for Sly is to be the best damn band in the world," Billy reminded them.

"Sly himself said that," Pres added. "In that letter he sent us."

Sam took a thoughtful bite of her ice cream. "Have you heard anything else from him?" she asked.

"He called us yesterday," Billy said.

"Billy told him about the tour," Pres related as he reached for his coffee cup and took a sip.

"What did he say?" Sam asked.

"He cried," Billy said simply.

Carrie felt tears come to her eyes. Billy noticed this, and reached for her hand to take it reassuringly.

"He was happy," Billy said quickly. "He was crying because he was happy for us. He said, 'Get that contract, Billy. Just get that contract.'"

"And I'm going to make sure we do get

that recording contract," Pres said, his voice steely, "if it's the last thing I do."

"For him," Billy said. "For Sly."

"Mmmm," Carrie whispered, "that's delicious."

"Better than dinner?" Billy asked her.

"Much," Carrie murmured, feeling Billy's lips on her cheek.

It was well after dinner. Carrie and Billy had made their way up to Billy's room after Pres and Sam had gone out together for a walk. They were lying on Billy's bed, their arms around each other. Carrie had taken off her vest and her shoes, and Billy had taken off his tux jacket, his shoes, and his bow tie.

Billy kissed Carrie's hair, then drew her closer and softly kissed her lips. The kisses grew hotter, until Carrie felt breathless and dizzy.

"Does this lovely dress unzip or what?" Billy asked, gently turning Carrie over.

"Or what," Carrie said with a chuckle. "It goes over my head."

Billy gently pulled Carrie into a sitting position, then lifted her dress over her head. She had on a white lace teddy, the one and only frilly undergarment she owned.

"Wow," Billy said huskily. He leaned over and kissed her shoulder.

"I guess that means you like it," Carrie said, feeling shy.

"Carrie, how can you be so gorgeous and so insecure about it?" Billy asked.

"Well, if you tell me I'm gorgeous for the next hundred years or so, I might get over it," Carrie replied softly.

"It's a deal," Billy agreed. He took her in his arms and kissed her again.

At that moment the phone rang.

"Just a sec," Billy said softly. He reached for the phone. "Hello?"

Carrie watched as Billy's face instantly changed. He stuck his hand over the receiver.

"It's my mother," Billy told her. "Get the lights, will you? And please find me a pen and paper."

Carrie did as Billy asked. She snapped on the light switch by the bed, and instantly Billy's room was filled with harsh yellow light. She saw a pen and a pad of paper over on his dresser, and brought them to him.

Suddenly Carrie felt stupid standing there in her underwear. She picked up her dress and slipped it back on.

"Uh-huh," Billy said, his voice growing edgier. "Uh-huh."

It seemed to Carrie that Billy said "uh-huh" a million times during that conversation with his mother. And all the while he was jotting stuff down on the paper she'd brought him—stuff that Carrie couldn't really read upside down.

"Mom," Billy said, "I can't do that—" He broke off and listened again. "Uh-huh," he said after a long interval. "Uh-huh."

Finally Carrie could stand it no longer. "What's the matter?" she hissed. Billy just waved to her to be silent.

"Uh-huh," he said again. "Okay. I'll call you later. Bye."

Billy hung up the phone. Carrie could see that he was trying to stay calm, but his right hand was shaking.

"What happened?" Carrie asked him, concerned.

"My father," Billy said quietly. "He's not doing so well."

· Carrie let out a quick breath. "I thought he was fine," she said.

"So did I," Billy replied. "So did I." He leaned back on the bed, his back against the headboard, and drummed his fingers on his knee nervously.

"What did she say?" Carrie asked, taking Billy's hand.

"He's been at home in bed with two leg casts since the accident. But she said he fell out of bed and hit his head on the bedpost—so hard he was knocked unconscious."

"Oh, Billy!" Carrie cried, putting her arms around him. "That's terrible!"

"No kidding," Billy said. "She called the ambulance, and they're at the hospital now."

"When did this happen?" Carrie asked.

"Now, obviously!" Billy yelled. He pulled away from Carrie and ran his hand through his hair. "I'm sorry," he said. "I shouldn't take it out on you."

"It's okay," she said soothingly. "I understand."

Silence.

"Maybe it's nothing," Carrie said softly.

"How can it be nothing, Carrie?" Billy asked. "The man was knocked unconscious!"

"Well, I meant maybe it isn't serious," Carrie said. She reached out for Billy and stroked his forehead. "Does that feel good?"

He didn't answer.

Carrie tried not to let the panic she was beginning to feel overwhelm her. "Whenever I stroke Chloe's forehead like this, it always calms her right down," she said, trying for a light tone.

But Billy was apparently in no mood for talk about Chloe. "Carrie, my mother wants me to come home. For good."

FIVE

I can't believe I'm actually doing this, Carrie thought as she paid her admission fee to the Sunset Island Psychic Fair for the second time.

It was the next afternoon. Billy had called Carrie first thing in the morning to report that the doctors in Seattle were doing a barrage of tests on his father, and that the results should be reported within twenty-four hours.

"I don't know what to do," he'd admitted. Carrie thought his voice sounded a little panic-stricken.

Carrie had to say that she didn't know what to do, either. With all her heart she had wanted to beg Billy not to go back to Seattle, but she knew she couldn't do that.

Instead she'd just told him that she loved him and hung up the phone.

And then it had hit her. *I'll go see Mrs. Ricci at the psychic fair,* she'd thought. *Look at all the things she told Emma. And if it turns out to be ridiculous, what am I out? Five dollars? No big deal.*

As long as I don't run into anyone I know.

So she'd done her morning's baby-sitting for Chloe, and then on her lunch hour hustled down to the psychic fair.

It was still in full swing, although Carrie could see when she went inside that there were far fewer people around than there had been on the weekend, when she'd been there with Emma and Sam.

I've got to do this quickly, she thought. *I'm with Chloe this afternoon again, and then I told Billy that I'd go to band practice later.*

She wended her way through the tables set up inside the main tent, looking for the one with Mrs. Ricci's name on it.

"Hey, Blue," Aura Man called out as she passed him. "You're back! And you're the same color!"

Carrie attempted a smile and continued to look for Mrs. Ricci.

"I have to read you!" Aura Man cried, running over to her. "I don't see an aura like yours every day!"

"Really?" Carrie asked dubiously. "So exactly how often do you see one like mine?"

Aura Man looked injured. "No two auras are alike, man," he said. "Which means I've never seen one like yours."

"So in other words, you're just trying to get me to spend some money," Carrie translated sharply.

Aura Man took a step away from her. "Bad vibes, man, seriously bad vibes. If you're such a cynic, what are you doing here?"

"I'm asking myself the same question," Carrie mumbled. "Excuse me." She continued to wander up and down the rows, looking for Mrs. Ricci.

Okay, I feel like an idiot, she said to herself. *And if I don't find this Mrs. Ricci soon, I'm turning right around and trucking out of here.*

Finally Carrie found Mrs. Ricci's table.

But Mrs. Ricci wasn't there.

Instead, there was a hand-printed note taped to the chair.

To my clients:

I am spending the early portion of this afternoon at the beach. I shall certainly return for readings and consultations after three o'clock this afternoon.

Mrs. Ricci

Carrie laughed out loud when she read the note. *I can't blame her for going to the beach,* she thought. *It's probably where I ought to be, too.*

But for some reason she continued to wander the aisles of the fair, looking for someone who might be able to give her some advice about her worries about Billy.

A friendly voice called out to her as she passed one table. "Miss? Can I help you?"

Carrie turned to the voice. It was a tiny older woman, about sixty, Carrie guessed. She was wearing a black dress and had a crocheted shawl wrapped around her shoulders. Her blue eyes twinkled as she smiled at Carrie. The sign on her desk read ANNIE ANDERSON, OUIJA SPECIALIST.

Ouija specialist? Carrie thought. *Meaning she reads a Ouija board? Give me a break!*

"Oh, I don't think so," Carrie said politely. "Thanks, anyway."

"I can tell you're troubled," the older woman called to Carrie. "I want to help."

Carrie took a tentative step toward her. "I wouldn't say troubled, exactly. . . ."

"Yes, yes, you are," Annie Anderson said, her brow furrowed. "I see deep concerns, decisions to make."

"I guess you could say that about anyone," Carrie pointed out, but she didn't move away.

"I could," Annie allowed, "but we're talking about you right now. I can help."

"I don't think so."

"Sit down," Annie urged, still smiling, "and we'll see what we can do."

"Just a sec," Carrie said, hesitating. "How much is a reading?"

"I don't do readings," Annie said as she

bent over and picked a Ouija board up off the floor. "I just channel spirits through this board."

"Yeah, right," Carrie said.

Annie raised her eyebrows. "You're a doubter?"

"I suppose you could call me a healthy cynic," Carrie said. "I don't want to offend you or anything, but . . ."

"No, I'm not offended in the least," Annie said. "It's healthy and smart to be wary of charlatans—there are so many around."

"There really are!" Carrie agreed.

"But some of us are real," the older woman said quietly. "Some of us—not many, but some—have a gift. A gift we need to share with others."

"How much will it cost?" Carrie asked again.

"Ten dollars for fifteen minutes," Annie said. "That's my student rate—you look like a student."

"I am," Carrie replied, settling into the chair across from Annie. She took a ten-dollar bill out of her wallet and placed it on the table. "At Yale."

"Yale?" Annie asked. "Great school! I went to Princeton myself."

"Princeton?" Carrie asked. "Really?"

"No," Annie admitted, "but it sounds better than Penn State."

Carrie laughed. *At least Annie has a sense of humor,* she thought.

Annie settled the Ouija board so that it rested on both her knees and Carrie's knees.

"I always thought a Ouija board was just for fun," Carrie said as she watched Annie set it up.

"In the hands of some, perhaps," Annie agreed. "You know how this board works?" she asked.

"I think so," Carrie said. "We put our fingers on the slippery planchette, right?"

"Right," Annie said, "our fingertips." She placed her fingertips on the planchette, and Carrie did the same. "I'll help channel the energy to give you your answers. We'll read the letters through the glass in this little plastic planchette."

The planchette began to move slowly on the board.

"Quick," Annie said, "think of your question for the spirits!"

Carrie closed her eyes. *Please,* she thought, *please tell me the right thing to do with Billy.*

The planchette moved faster on the board. Carrie couldn't tell for sure, but it felt as if Annie was helping to push the planchette.

It came to a stop on the number 1. And then the number 9. And then the number 8. And the number 0.

"1980," Annie said. "An important year."

"How so?" Carrie asked, puzzled.

"You know the answer to that," Annie told her.

"I don't," Carrie answered, her fingertips still on the now lifeless planchette. "Honestly, I don't."

"Well, why don't you ask the board?" Annie prompted her.

"Okay," Carrie said skeptically. She concentrated on the planchette. It started to move.

She's moving it, Carrie thought as the planchette started to move again on the board. *I know she's moving it around!*

Quickly Carrie pulled her fingertips off the planchette, so only Annie's hands were on it. The planchette should have stopped moving if it was being controlled by the spirits. Instead, the heart-shaped plastic planchette flew off the Ouija board and into Carrie's lap.

Aha! Carrie thought. *She was moving it all the time. What a rip-off!*

"Powerful spirits!" Annie exclaimed. "They pulled your fingers off!"

Carrie shook her head. "I don't think so," she said as she got up to leave.

"Wait!" Annie said. "We're just starting to get at the answers! The spirits get very angry if you turn your back on them!"

"Right," Carrie said with a sigh, picking up her purse.

"But I have answers!" Annie protested. "You could come to great harm if you walk away now!"

The kind of answers you're giving me are worse than the questions, Carrie thought. *When can I get to see Mrs. Ricci?*

"Billy says his dad probably has a subdural hematoma," Carrie explained as she, Emma, and Sam walked slowly along the beach.

"A what?" Sam asked.

"Subdural hematoma," Carrie repeated.

"Sounds horrible," Sam commented, kicking the lapping waves of the ocean as she walked along.

"I know," Carrie agreed with a sigh.

It was nearly dark. The girls had all gone to a band rehearsal together at five, and the rehearsal broke up unexpectedly early, at six-thirty.

"I can't do this now," Billy had said, shaking his head as he unslung his guitar in the middle of a song.

Pres and the other band members had remonstrated with him and reminded him that no matter what, they had to get ready for the Maine mini-tour that was coming up.

"I don't care," Billy had mumbled. "Not now!"

"C'mon, man," Pres had drawled, "just put it aside for an hour."

"Easy for you to say," Billy had snapped, and then he had gone upstairs. No one knew what to do or say. Pres finally stormed out of the room.

Eventually Carrie had followed Billy upstairs, but Billy had—nicely—told her

82

that he just wanted to be alone for a while. She had slowly come back downstairs, feeling scared and anxious.

That had effectively ended rehearsal, so Sam, Emma, and Carrie decided to go for a stroll on the beach. Now they were walking together in the early twilight. The beach was quiet except for some municipal four-wheel-drive vehicles that were busy cleaning up the day's trash from the usual crowd of sun worshipers.

"So, what is this subdural thing, anyway?" Sam asked, pushing some hair behind her ear.

"It's bleeding in the brain, Sam," Emma said. "I remember reading about it in bio."

Carrie nodded. "That's right," she said.

"When there's blood between layers of membrane just under the skull," Emma continued, reaching over to pick up a pretty reddish shell, "it puts pressure on the brain."

"That can have some pretty serious consequences," Carrie said.

"Usually they operate," Emma said softly.

"That's right," Carrie agreed. "Brain surgery. To relieve the pressure."

"God," Sam breathed, "that's terrible. What's Billy going to do?"

"His mother wants him to come home," Carrie said, dancing away from an incoming wave.

"He can't do that!" Sam cried. "What about the tour?"

"His family comes first . . . I guess," Emma commented.

Carrie shrugged. "I don't know what he's going to decide. All I know is that I'm all mixed up!" She reached down, picked up a shell of her own, and tossed it absentmindedly back into the ocean.

"Spill your guts," Sam advised her. "We're here to confuse you more."

Carrie grinned weakly.

"You don't have to talk about it if you don't want to," Emma advised her.

Carrie stopped and gazed at the ocean. "I don't know what I want," she said finally.

"You want him to stay," Sam said, sitting down on the ground. "He's your love."

"You want him to go," Emma said as she

sat down next to Sam, "because it's his father."

"You want to go with him," Sam suggested, "because you don't want to be apart from him."

"You'll never go to Seattle," Emma commented. "What about Yale? What about your own dreams?"

Carrie smiled and joined her friends on the sand. "That just about sums it up, doesn't it?"

"Samantha Bridges, psychic advisor to the stars," Sam quipped.

"With her psychic helper, Emma Cresswell," Emma said.

All three girls laughed.

Just then they saw another girl running toward them along the waterline. She was dressed in a plain gray pair of sweatpants and a loose blue jersey, and she was barefoot. Her long dark hair was held back by a white cotton headband.

"Darcy!" Sam exclaimed as the girl grew closer. "How's the girl jock of the century?"

Their friend slowed to a walk and put her hands up over her head, breathing almost normally.

"Hanging in there," Darcy said. She dropped to the sand next to Sam.

"I hate you," Sam said.

"How come?" Darcy asked.

"How far did you run?" Sam asked accusingly.

"About three miles," Darcy replied.

"And you're not even breathing hard!" Sam cried.

"Oh, cut it out, Sam," Emma said with a smile. "You're a dancer. You practice every day. You're in great shape, too."

Sam pouted. "I know. I just like to yank Darcy's chain." She looked up at Darcy and laughed. "But I guess I'm busted now."

Darcy laughed, too. "Sorry, Sam. Next time." Then she changed the subject. "I'm glad I ran into you guys." She looked past Sam, straight at Carrie. "Actually, I had a dream about you last night."

Carrie came to attention. Sometimes Darcy's dreams turned out to be eerily accurate. If Darcy had dreamed about her, she wanted to know what it was all about.

"Really?" Carrie asked.

"Yup," Darcy said.

"So what did you dream?" Sam asked.

86

Darcy adjusted the sweatband on her head. "Remember that just because I have a dream doesn't mean it necessarily means anything."

"But you have ESP!" Emma said.

"Not always," Darcy reminded her. "I mean, sometimes I have normal dreams just like everyone else."

"So which kind was this?" Sam asked.

Darcy sighed. "Who knows? I can't tell them apart. But this one felt . . . I don't know. Significant."

Carrie nodded seriously. "Please tell me."

"All right," Darcy said quietly. "You were lost."

"Lost?" Carrie echoed.

"On a road," Darcy explained. "Lost at a huge intersection. You were running around and crying."

"Sounds sort of real," Carrie mused aloud.

"Does it remind you of anything?" Darcy asked Carrie.

Carrie shook her head. "Do *you* know what it means?"

"No," Darcy admitted. "It just seemed like you didn't know which way to turn."

"Then what happened?" Carrie asked, a chill running inexplicably up her spine as Darcy talked.

"Some older woman appeared," Darcy said, a note of puzzlement in her voice. "I don't know who it was."

"What did this woman do?" Carrie asked, already guessing what Darcy might say.

"She helped you," Darcy replied. "She got you on the right road."

Mrs. Ricci! Carrie thought. *That older woman in Darcy's dream is Mrs. Ricci. She's got the answers. I feel it. All those other so-called psychics were fakes, but Mrs. Ricci is the real thing, and now Darcy's dream has proven it. I've got to see her.*

"Carrie?" Darcy asked. "You okay? You look a little lost."

Carrie's eyes shone brightly. "I know who the older woman is," she said quietly. "And she *is* going to help me. I just know it."

SIX

"You say your name is Carrie?" Mrs. Ricci said as she looked closely at her. Carrie suddenly got the strangest feeling, as if Mrs. Ricci was actually staring into her soul.

"Yes," Carrie said. "Carrie Alden."

"Well, Carrie Alden," Mrs. Ricci said disarmingly, reaching a hand across the table, "it's nice to meet you."

"I hope you can help me," Carrie said, automatically shaking Mrs. Ricci's hand. It felt warm, dry, and somehow very comforting.

"So do I," Mrs. Ricci said with a little laugh. "So do I."

It was almost noon the next day. Carrie had called Billy as soon as she'd gotten up.

No, Billy had told her, they hadn't gotten the final results yet on his father's tests, but it still looked like a subdural hematoma.

And yes, Billy had said, his mother still wanted him to go back to Seattle. Right away.

"So what are you going to do?" Carrie had asked Billy, dreading his answer.

"I don't know," Billy had replied with a sigh.

"Even if you went home, you wouldn't stay for good, like your mother wants, would you?" Carrie had asked.

"Look, Car, I don't know anything right now," Billy had said, an edge to his voice.

She hadn't pressed him any further.

I need help, Carrie had thought. *A lot of help. Darcy's dream yesterday was dead on—I feel lost, as if I'm running around with no idea what to do. I need to see Mrs. Ricci. Today.*

Fortunately, Carrie had the entire day free—Graham and Claudia had taken the entire family to Old Orchard Beach to celebrate Ian's having gotten his song on the soundtrack. That night the Zits were going to rehearse at the Templetons' house, and Ian had confided to Carrie that he was going to give Becky Jacobs the big boot.

"She deserves it," Ian had said at breakfast, trying to sound confident. Carrie, her mind on other things, had just nodded distractedly.

"I mean, look at what she did to me!" Ian had continued. "She, like, totally used me! First we were this big couple, then she just dropped me. Well, if she can drop me, I can drop her from my band, right?"

Carrie had nodded again, not really listening. Ian's problems with Becky seemed like nothing compared to her own.

And now she was sitting for the third time that week in the main tent of the Sunset Island Psychic Fair, this time actually across from the elusive Mrs. Ricci.

Emma's right, Carrie thought as she took in Mrs. Ricci's totally ordinary looks. *She looks like someone you'd see at the bus stop or in the grocery.*

Mrs. Ricci was middle-aged and slightly overweight. She had brown hair streaked with a bit of gray, and she wore gray pants with a navy blue cotton sweater.

"So, Carrie Alden," Mrs. Ricci said, a broad smile crossing her face, "what's your birthday?"

"What's your fee?"

Mrs. Ricci laughed gently. "I'll do the reading, then you pay me either five dollars or what you think I'm worth. Fair enough?"

"Fair enough," Carrie agreed, feeling nervous.

"So, what's your birthday?"

Carrie told her.

"How about when you were born?"

"What do you mean?" Carrie asked, puzzled.

"When, as in what time," Mrs. Ricci asked.

"Oh!" Carrie said, now comprehending. "Five o'clock in the morning. In New York City. Mount Sinai Hospital, actually."

Mrs. Ricci laughed. "Five o'clock in the morning? You're an early bird!"

Carrie smiled. She was feeling too anxious and stressed out to actually laugh.

"All right," Mrs. Ricci said, "let's see what the stars say, shall we?"

Carrie watched as she took out a couple

of overstuffed looseleaf notebooks and flipped through them, jotting some notes down on a yellow legal pad. Finally she looked up at Carrie.

"You're a scholar," she said matter-of-factly. "What's your GPA?"

"My GPA?" Carrie said in wonder, not expecting her grades at Yale to be the first topic of conversation. "Three point seven five."

"You got a B in a foreign language?" Mrs. Ricci asked.

Carrie was stunned. *How could she have known that I got a B in my Spanish class?*

"Spanish," Carrie admitted.

"Study harder," Mrs. Ricci advised. "Foreign languages don't come easily to you."

That was accurate, too. Carrie felt a shudder roll through her. "I'll try," she promised.

Mrs. Ricci looked down at her legal pad again. "You feel a lot of pressure from your parents," she reported.

"That's true," Carrie said, feeling dazed. "Very true."

"You like them, but you think you have

93

to be perfect for them," Mrs. Ricci continued.

"Yes, exactly," Carrie agreed. "How did you know?"

Mrs. Ricci tapped her notebooks. "These don't lie," she said simply. She studied the notebooks some more.

Out of the corner of her eye, Carrie could see people walking back and forth past the table where she was sitting with Mrs. Ricci, but for the moment Carrie felt as if she and Mrs. Ricci were in their own little world.

"Let me tell you a few other things," Mrs. Ricci finally said, looking up again. "You're a true and loyal friend, but you don't have lots of friends. I see two friends, very, very close, more like sisters."

"Emma and Sam!" Carrie cried.

"Let me tell you some other things I see," Mrs. Ricci said. And then she proceeded to launch into a five-minute monologue about Carrie, her family, her friends on the island, and her romantic history that left Carrie absolutely dumbfounded.

"You're amazing," Carrie declared when Mrs. Ricci was finished. Any skepticism that she had had about astrology and psychics had totally vanished.

"Thanks," Mrs. Ricci said.

"I really didn't believe in any of this before," Carrie continued in a rush. "I was beginning to think everyone here at this fair was just a fraud."

"Many are," Mrs. Ricci agreed.

"But not you," Carrie said. "Really, I'm so impressed!"

Mrs. Ricci smiled. "I have a bit of psychic advice for you."

"What's that?" Carrie asked seriously, leaning closer.

"Stay away from Aura Man," Mrs. Ricci advised, her voice dropping nearly to a whisper. "He was in jail for writing bad checks."

Carrie laughed, feeling much better. "Have you ever thought about doing stand-up comedy?" she asked.

"Too much like work," Mrs. Ricci said. "Besides, the hours are lousy. Now, is there anything specific I can help you with?"

"Yes," Carrie said gratefully. "It's really the reason I came to see you." She shifted uneasily in her seat. "See, I have this major problem." She opened her purse and reached for a Kennedy half-dollar her mother had given her on her fifth birthday.

If there's anything I have that has psychic energy in it, Carrie had thought earlier, *it's that half-dollar. Because it's amazing I never spent it.*

"Ah," Mrs. Ricci said, seeing Carrie take the money out of her bag, "you don't think my reading is worth much."

Carrie hastened to explain. "No, it's—"

Mrs. Ricci laughed a hearty laugh. "I'm only joking with you," she said. "You must have had a friend visit me before."

"Emma Cresswell," Carrie admitted. "She told me you like to hold something personal of the person you're doing the reading for."

"Well," Mrs. Ricci said, reaching for the coin, "hand it over."

Carrie placed the half-dollar in Mrs. Ricci's hand, and watched as the woman closed her eyes.

"What's the question?" she asked, her eyes still closed.

Carrie hesitated. *Am I really going to do this? I can't believe I am!*

"My boyfriend, Billy," Carrie began, her voice faltering. "His father is in the hospital."

"They're not sure," Mrs. Ricci said flatly, screwing her eyes shut even more tightly. "They're not exactly sure. . . ."

"Not sure what's wrong?" Carrie asked.

"Something with the brain," the psychic said. "It's serious."

"Will he be okay?"

"The doctors don't agree on the prognosis," Mrs. Ricci said slowly. "I see disagreement, a lack of harmony. Is your boyfriend here?"

"Yes," Carrie said quickly. "On the island."

"His mother wants him home," Mrs. Ricci said. "Soon. Now."

"I know," Carrie said. "But—"

"He'll go," Mrs. Ricci continued. "He's a good boy. Very good."

"I know."

"Don't lose him," Mrs. Ricci said, her eyes opening. "Don't lose him, Carrie. His father will live, but you could lose Billy. Don't let it happen."

Carrie felt as if someone had punched her in the stomach.

"Are . . . are you sure?" Carrie whispered.

Mrs. Ricci patted Carrie's hand. "I don't give guarantees, dear. I only tell you what I see or feel."

"So what should I do?" Carrie asked, distraught.

Mrs. Ricci smiled kindly and handed Carrie back her half-dollar. "Some things, dear, even the stars cannot answer."

But I know the answer anyway, Carrie thought, gulping hard. *She's telling me to go to Seattle. If I don't, I could lose Billy forever.*

"I wussed out," Ian Templeton said, hanging his head sadly as he trudged into the kitchen.

The Zits had just finished their rehearsal. And Ian was supposed to have kicked Becky Jacobs out of the band.

Carrie was sitting there alone, waiting for Billy to come over, flipping idly through a book of photographs by Ed Clark, the renowned former photographer for *Life* magazine. She'd found herself staring at one in particular. Taken in the 1950s, it showed two migrant farmworker girls, both around twelve years old, sitting together.

I wonder what their hopes and dreams were, Carrie thought, staring at the wonderful photograph. *And I wonder whatever happened to them. Were they ever so in love with a boy that they thought they would die if he went away, that they'd do anything not to lose him?*

She closed her eyes and sighed. *This isn't me,* she thought. *I have a whole plan for my life, and following Billy to Seattle isn't part of it. But if he goes, maybe he'll convince his mom he doesn't need to stay forever. Maybe it will only be for a few days. Maybe everything will work out and we can—*

"Hey, Car, did you hear what I said?" Ian said loudly, interrupting Carrie's thoughts.

"What?" Carrie said, focusing on him.

Ian looked at Carrie crossly. "Didn't you hear me? I said I wussed out! About Becky!"

"You mean you didn't—"

"Nope," Ian said, slumping into a chair

near Carrie's. "I wanted to, but the other guys in the band told me they'd quit if I did it."

"Pressure," Carrie said sympathetically.

"They called it advice!" Ian grumbled. "They said they like having the girls in the band. They said it gives us class because the twins are babes! They said if I kicked Becky out, Allie would leave, too."

"Well, maybe they have a point," Carrie counseled him, happy for a change to be thinking about something less important than her problems with Billy.

"Are you kidding?" Ian asked, looking at Carrie askance. "Do you think The Who had girls in the band? Did the Beatles? What about Neil Young?"

"Neil Young is just one guy," Carrie reminded Ian. "Hey, even your father has used backup singers."

"Rarely!" Ian maintained. "Only rarely!" He reached for a bunch of grapes in the fruit bowl on the table and popped one in his mouth.

"Think of it this way," Carrie said. "When you're singing your new song—the one about Becky—you can sing it right to her, because she's right there."

Ian looked at Carrie, and it was as if a lightbulb had gone on in his head. "Yeah," he said softly. "I never thought of that."

"So, that might be good, right?" Carrie asked.

"If she gets the message," Ian said. He scratched his chin thoughtfully. "Do you think I should pierce my ear?"

"Gee, Ian, I don't know. . . ."

"Or maybe my eyebrow," Ian continued. "Or my tongue."

Carrie shuddered. "That's awful, Ian."

"But what if—"

Just then the doorbell rang. "Excuse me, Ian," Carrie said. "I think that's Billy." She got up to answer the door.

"Hey, thanks for the advice, Carrie!" Ian called after her. "I'm gonna go practice."

"Don't pierce anything for a while!" she called back to him. *Great,* Carrie thought as she headed for the hall. *I'm a genius when it comes to Ian's problems. Why is it that I'm totally lost when it comes to my own?*

"Damn it, Carrie," Billy said, slamming his hand down on the kitchen table. "I don't have a choice, can't you see that?"

"You do have a choice," Carrie pointed out. "You're making it."

Billy slumped down in his chair. "Why now?" he asked, looking up at the ceiling as if he were trying to talk to God. "Why now? Of all times, why now?"

The ceiling didn't answer him.

It was twenty minutes after Billy had arrived, and it had been twenty minutes of bad news. Billy reported that his dad did indeed have a subdural hematoma, that he had undergone brain surgery at the University of Washington Medical Center in Seattle, and that there had been some complications with his recovery.

"There are tubes draining fluid from beneath his skull," Billy had said, "and they're draining more than the doctors want to see."

It didn't take long for Billy to get to his point. He was going back to Seattle right away. For how long, he didn't know. He hoped it would be for a short time. He hoped his mother would understand that he needed to be on Sunset Island. And then he got to the part that Carrie had been praying she wasn't going to hear.

"Carrie," Billy said softly, "I really want you to come with me. Just for a while."

"I'm glad you want me," Carrie said softly.

"I sense a *but* coming," Billy said.

Carrie stared at the table. "I don't know what to say."

"Say yes," Billy urged her. "Just say yes."

That's what Mrs. Ricci would tell me to say, Carrie thought. *What am I hesitating for? For a million reasons, that's what for!*

"There's my job," Carrie began.

Billy reached for the glass of Coke that Carrie had poured him earlier. "C'mon, Car," he said. "Graham and Claudia would understand. You know they would."

"Maybe," Carrie said. "But for how long? I wouldn't even be able to tell them that."

"We'd call with updates," Billy said.

"And they're supposed to just hang on, not knowing when I'm coming back?" Carrie asked. *Or if I'm coming back,* she added to herself.

"The uncertainty will be over soon," Billy said. "And then we'd make some decisions."

"But . . . but . . . but what about money?" Carrie asked, feeling a ball of panic bouncing around the pit of her stomach.

"Look, Car, it's not a problem. We'd be staying with my family, so there are no expenses. And it would probably only be for a little while."

"Really?" Carrie asked.

"Probably just a week or two."

"Are you sure?" Carrie asked, her eyes searching his. "Are you totally sure about that?"

"No," Billy admitted. "I'm not totally sure."

"That's what I thought," Carrie mumbled. *Great,* she thought. *If I stay here, I might come out of this with no boyfriend. What if it turns out his mom really needs him and he has to stay in Seattle? What then? What am I going to do?*

"It depends on my father," Billy said.

Carrie looked up at the ceiling, as Billy had done earlier. "Why now?" she asked. "Why?"

"My family needs me," Billy said earnestly. "I can't just turn my back on them. You know I can't!"

Carrie put her hand on top of Billy's on the table. "I know," she said softly. "I'd do the same as you."

"Then come with me!" Billy urged her. "I've booked two seats on the two o'clock flight to Chicago tomorrow. Then we change for Seattle."

"What if it turns out that you do have to stay there?" Carrie asked him. "What about the Flirts? What about us?"

"You could stay, too," Billy replied softly. Then he added with more enthusiasm, "You'd love it there!"

Carrie pulled her hand away from his. "How can you say that, as if it's all so simple and easy?" she cried. "I'd be turning my life inside out! What about college?"

"You think there aren't colleges in Seattle?" Billy said, his voice rising.

"But this is crazy!" Carrie cried. "You just told me we'd only go for a week or two!"

"I also told you I'm not sure."

Carrie's hands flew to her hair. "Oh, God, Billy, I don't know what to do! What about Yale?"

"There are good schools in Seattle," Billy

said. "There's the University of Washington, for one. You can go there."

"What about my family?" Carrie asked.

"What about *my* family?" Billy shouted. "My family is the one in trouble now!"

The two of them looked at each other. Carrie drew in a deep breath. "Billy, I . . . I don't know what to say."

"Say you love me," he said in a low voice. "Say that you'll be there for me."

"I do love you," Carrie insisted. "I love you so much. . . ."

"When you love someone, sometimes you have to make tough decisions."

Carrie bit her lip. "If it were all reversed, would you give up everything to follow me to New Jersey?"

Billy blinked for a moment. "I hope so," he finally said. He looked out the window. "I remember when your friend was going to be deported unless you married him. I remember thinking I was going to lose you."

"Oh, that was so awful," Carrie recalled.

"I think that's when I realized just how much I love you, when I really knew that I couldn't bear to lose you," Billy said. "That nothing would have any meaning in my life without you." He looked back at Carrie. "I can't tell you what to do, Car. But I can tell you how much it would mean to me if you come with me."

Carrie waited a long time before she said anything. And finally she told Billy the truth.

"I'm not sure," she whispered. "I'm just not sure."

Which left them exactly nowhere.

SEVEN

"You're asking an awful lot," Graham said as he regarded Carrie's anxious face across the breakfast table.

"Yeah," Ian piped up. "He's only going to hurt you in the long run."

"Ian!" Claudia snapped from over at the sink, where she was rinsing the breakfast dishes. "That's quite enough from you, thank you."

"It's true!" Ian cried. "Love always does that! Billy's gonna hurt her! Love stinks!"

"That's not true," Claudia said.

"Says who?" Ian challenged.

"Says me," Claudia replied. "Your father and I love each other very much."

"Yeah, but lots of my friends' parents are

divorced—some more than once," Ian reminded her. "So what makes you think that—"

"Yo, Ian, chill," Graham interrupted his son. "Maybe it'd be best if you left us alone for a little while with Carrie."

"But—"

"We'll have your discussion another time," Graham told him firmly.

"But—"

"Now!" Graham repeated, losing his patience.

Ian scowled, but slowly got up from the breakfast table, made a face that only Carrie could see, and left the room.

After her argument with Billy the night before, Carrie had gone to bed. But she hadn't really slept. As she'd tossed and turned she'd thought about what Mrs. Ricci had told her, and she'd thought about Darcy's dream.

And finally she'd made a decision.

I'm going to go with Billy to Seattle, Carrie thought. *That is, if Graham and Claudia will let me. I'm going to go for a few days. Maybe that will be enough for*

Billy and his mother, and we can both come back to the island. If not, I'll cross that bridge when we come to it.

I'm sure that's exactly what Mrs. Ricci would advise me to do.

She had just explained the whole story about Billy's father to her employers, and had asked Graham and Claudia for five days off so she could make the trip. That would give her and Billy three full days in Seattle to visit his father.

Graham and Claudia weren't happy about the idea at all. Not a bit.

"So, Carrie," Claudia said to her, walking back over to the kitchen table, "who's going to take care of the kids while you're away?"

"Well, I thought that since it's only a few days, maybe you could get by. . . ."

"It's very short notice—you want to leave this afternoon!—and I have a lot of things to do over the next few days," Claudia said patiently.

"And I'm going to be in the studio recording some tracks," Graham put in, "so you know I won't be around much."

"You were already talking about wanting some time off so you could take photos during the Flirts' tour," Claudia added. "Now you're asking us to more than double the amount of time off we're giving you."

"I don't even know what's going to happen with the tour now," Carrie said despondently. She took a deep breath to calm herself down. "I know I'm asking for a lot," she went on in even tones. "And I wouldn't ask if Billy's dad weren't so ill."

"If he's that ill, it sounds like it will take more than five days," Claudia pointed out gently.

"I won't be gone more than that," Carrie replied. "I give you my word."

Graham fiddled with a pencil. "I guess we can work it out," he finally said. "Billy's a great guy, and I know you and he have gotten really tight."

"It's easy for you to say it will work out, Graham," Claudia told him. "You know you won't be home to look after the kids."

"So we'll hire someone to help you for a few days, if that's what you need," Graham said.

"Since when is it any more my responsibility than yours?" Claudia wondered.

Graham began to say something and then apparently thought better of it. He turned back to Carrie. "Look, we'll manage here for the next five days. But after that we'll need you to work according to the schedule we originally agreed upon, okay?"

"Yes, absolutely," Carrie assured him. "And thank you. Thank you both, so much!"

Claudia managed to smile at her. "It's all right, Carrie. Believe me, we can see how important this is to you, and you know we think the world of you. We're just not used to managing without you anymore!"

Carrie smiled back. "I'll be back soon."

Claudia reached out and put her hand on Carrie's. "We hope Billy's dad is okay."

"Thanks," Carrie said, her voice shaky. "More than you know."

"What time are you leaving?" Claudia asked her.

"We have a one o'clock flight from Portland to Chicago," Carrie reported. "We change planes there for Seattle."

"Good luck," Graham said quietly.

Carrie smiled and thanked Graham and Claudia once again, but she was thinking that it wasn't she who needed the good luck—it was Billy's father.

Because if he didn't get better, then a lot of people's lives might change. . . .

Carrie stared out the window of the Northwest Airlines jet as it cruised along at thirty-three thousand feet over the state of Montana.

At least that's what the captain of the airplane had announced on the intercom. Actually, Carrie could see nothing but an unbroken blanket of white below them. Even though the sun was shining brightly into the airplane, the captain had explained that it was raining on the ground.

Billy was asleep in the seat next to her, his head on Carrie's shoulder.

What a day, Carrie thought. *What a day! And we're not even in Seattle yet.*

She was bone tired from not having slept the night before—so tired that her eyes hurt. But her mind was still racing at a thousand miles an hour, and at the moment was going back over the events that had led to her being on this airplane.

First the talk with Graham and Claudia, she recalled. *Then Billy's call, and how happy he was that I said yes. Then packing, and calling Emma and Sam to tell them what I was doing. Then Pres driving the two of us to Portland to get on this plane.*

And now I'm really doing it. I can't believe it.

One thing that Carrie hadn't done was call her parents in New Jersey to tell them that she'd be away from the island for a few days.

I don't want them to worry, she'd told herself. *Actually, I'm not sure they'd be very happy about my going to Seattle with Billy, especially if they knew that I don't know how long I'll be there. If they even thought there was a possibility that I wouldn't be going back to Yale, they'd probably drag me home by my hair.*

Carrie looked down at the fashion magazine she'd been trying to read. Her eyes lit on the horoscope section, and she scanned it quickly until she came to her birth sign.

TAURUS (April 20 – May 20):
Last-minute decision-making won't
make you as nervous as it sometimes does because you're ready
and willing to take action. Go
ahead and do what you've got to
do—you've figured out all the
angles.

I wish, Carrie thought. *I don't even know
what all the angles are.*

"Hey," Billy said softly as he rubbed his
eyes sleepily. "Wow, I had the most awful
dream."

"Are you okay?" Carrie asked in a soft
voice, taking his hand in her own.

"I'm not sure," he said, shaking his head.
"I mean, it was just so vivid."

"Tell me," Carrie murmured.

"I dreamed my father died," Billy confided quietly. "While we were right here on
this plane."

"Oh, Billy—"

He rubbed his hand over his face. "It felt
so real!"

"I'm sure he's okay," Carrie said. "You're
just anxious."

"How can you be sure?" Billy asked, sounding stressed. "You don't know!"

"No, I can't be sure," Carrie admitted.

Billy stared out the window. "It really spooked me, Car."

She tried to think of something comforting to say, and then she remembered the flight attendant announcing that their plane was equipped with an airphone.

"Listen," Carrie suggested, "if you're worried, why don't you call the hospital?"

"From here?" Billy asked dubiously.

Carrie got up, took his hand and, after asking the flight attendant where it was, led Billy to the airphone—an air-to-ground telephone that used the same kind of system cellular phones employed. "Go ahead, use it," she urged him.

"It'll cost a fortune," he demurred.

Carrie reached into her pocketbook, took out the MasterCard her parents had given her for emergencies, and handed it to Billy.

Billy took it reluctantly. "I'll pay you back," he promised.

"Okay," Carrie said. "You can pay me back."

Billy reached into his own wallet for a

piece of paper on which he'd written the number of the University of Washington Medical Center. He swiped the credit card down the slot provided for it, waited for a dial tone and then dialed some numbers.

"Sixth-floor nurses' station," he said tersely into the phone. Carrie watched him as he waited.

"Uh, this is Billy Sampson," he said when someone picked up. "I'm Frank Sampson's son. I'm calling to check on him."

Carrie took Billy's free hand and squeezed it tightly while he waited for word.

"What?" Billy said into the phone.

"What is it?" Carrie asked, concerned.

"Shhh!" Billy shushed her. "Say that again?" he said into the phone. "You're kidding. . . . You're not kidding? When did this happen? How come?"

There was more silence.

"Thank you," Billy said, his voice sounding dead. He hung the phone back up.

"What is it? What is it?" Carrie asked him worriedly.

Billy answered in the same monotone. "My dad's back in surgery," he reported. "Right now. He went in three hours ago."

* * *

"Billy!" a woman shouted.

"Mom!" Billy cried. He ran over and embraced the woman who had just come into the intensive-care waiting area at the hospital.

Carrie rose from the cushioned chair in which she'd been seated.

"How's Dad?" Billy asked quickly.

"We don't know yet," the woman said to Billy. "All we know is that he's alive."

"Thank God," Billy replied, still holding his mother. "Thank God."

"Thank God is right," the woman said. "I'm so glad you're finally here."

It was four hours later. Billy and Carrie's plane had arrived at the airport a little after six o'clock local time, and a friend of Billy's family had been waiting for them.

The friend—a rough-hewn man named Bill Tate, who told Carrie he'd known Billy's dad since his own days in the military— had driven the two of them directly from the airport to the University of Washington Medical Center and dropped them off,

119

promising that he'd take their luggage to Billy's family's home in west Seattle and leave it there.

The front desk at the hospital had directed them to the intensive-care unit.

Shyly Carrie approached Billy and his mom. For a second, coming into the hospital, she wished she'd worn something more elaborate to travel in than a plain pair of black summer shorts with a long-sleeved turquoise T-shirt. But when she saw Billy's mom in her faded plaid shorts and plain white shirt, she was glad she was dressed so simply.

"Hello," she began, "I'm—"

Billy cut her off gently. "I'm sorry," he said, putting his arm around Carrie's shoulders. "Mom, this is my girlfriend, Carrie Alden. Carrie, my mother, Grace Sampson."

Billy's mom was a slender, attractive woman with short gray hair. At the moment she looked exhausted and pale, with a web of fine lines around her anxious-looking eyes.

But Billy doesn't look anything like her, Carrie thought. *He must look like his dad.*

Carrie reached out to shake Billy's mother's hand. "I'm glad to meet you, Mrs. Sampson."

"Please," Grace Sampson said, "call me Grace. And I'm glad to meet you. I didn't know you were coming with Billy, but I'm happy you did."

Carrie shot Billy a look.

"I'm sorry," Billy said sheepishly. "I guess I got so stressed out I forgot to tell Mom you were coming."

"I'm sorry if it's an inconvenience," Carrie said, feeling very embarrassed.

"Not at all," Grace assured her. "From what Billy has told us about you, you pretty much walk on water." She gave Carrie a tired but warm smile. "Anyway, we're happy to have you."

"Thank you," Carrie murmured, blushing slightly. "I think a lot of Billy, too," she replied, gazing directly into Grace's weary blue eyes.

"So where is Dad?" Billy asked, taking Carrie's hand in his own.

"They just moved him from the recovery room to intensive care," his mother said.

"When can I see him?" Billy asked.

"Now," Grace Sampson said to her son. "If you want to."

"I want to," Billy replied. He turned to her. "Come on, Carrie."

Carrie hesitated.

This is the first time that he's going to see his father since this new crisis, she thought. *It's not like I'm his daughter-in-law yet or anything. I just feel funny.*

"It's okay," Billy said, as if he were reading her thoughts.

"I'll wait here," Carrie said, deciding to follow her instincts. "You go see him alone with your mom this time. I'll meet him tomorrow."

Grace gave her a grateful smile.

"You sure?" Billy asked her.

Carrie nodded. She glanced at Grace Sampson, and she saw a look of respect flit across Billy's mother's face.

"Okay, Billy James," Grace said, taking her son's arm and starting to lead him to the door. "Come on. Your father's waiting for us. And whatever else happens, don't you cry in front of him. And don't show

how alarmed you are about how bad he looks." She took a deep breath. "He's been to hell and back. But he's alive. He's still alive."

EIGHT

"Carrie?"

Is that Ian? Who's calling me? Carrie wondered, her mind half asleep and half awake. *Who's calling me? Can't they just let me sleep?*

"Carrie, wake up."

"Huh? Go away," Carrie mumbled.

"Carrie, wake up," the voice repeated.

Her eyes opened, and for a moment she had no idea where she was.

Then she saw Billy's familiar face near her cheek, and it all came back.

I'm in Billy's parents' house in Seattle, Carrie thought. *I'm really here. We were at the hospital last night to see his dad, and now I'm in his parents' house.*

"Hello, sleepyhead," Billy said with a big smile.

"Good morning," Carrie muttered sleepily.

"No, it's good afternoon," Billy corrected her. "Take a look at the clock."

Carrie glanced over at her travel alarm clock on the nightstand near her bed. It read 12:45 P.M.

"I slept," Carrie said with a wry smile.

"You slept, all right." Billy tousled her brown hair. "I stuck my head in at eleven, and you were still out like a light."

"I was whipped," Carrie said, groggily shaking her head. "I feel better now."

"Me, too," Billy reported. "And I'll feel better after I do this." He leaned over and gave her a delicious kiss on her lips.

"But I have morning breath!" she protested, laughing though the kiss.

"Not you," Billy teased. "You're a medical miracle."

Even though Carrie was still not totally awake, she returned the kiss warmly.

"This means I truly love you," Billy said solemnly. "I have kissed you before you brushed your teeth."

She threw a pillow at him. "Hey! I thought you just said my breath was okay!"

"I lied," Billy admitted, rubbing her shoulder.

"How's your dad?" Carrie asked, getting out of bed and putting a robe on over the long Sunset Island T-shirt she'd slept in.

"Better," Billy reported. "Mom called me from the hospital. He's still in intensive care, though. He's awake."

"You're sure it's okay if I see him later?" Carrie asked. "I don't want to intrude."

"He wants to meet you," Billy replied. "He said so last night."

"If you're sure . . ."

"I'm sure, Car," Billy said, pulling her close. "My whole family wants to get to know you. And when they do, they'll love you just as much as I do."

"When you say things like that I remember why I love you," Carrie said, giving him a hug. "I'm so glad your dad's better."

"You want coffee?" Billy asked her.

"Sure," Carrie said, starting for the door.

Billy pulled on her robe. "I came prepared." He reached for a thermos he'd brought upstairs with him, unscrewed the top, and poured Carrie a cup of hot steaming coffee.

"I wasn't sure you'd wake up," he explained, touching the thermos.

"This is great," Carrie said as she sat back down on the bed. "Hey, you make good coffee!"

"Service with a smile," Billy informed her. "Specialty of the house. Just a sec, I gotta go to the bathroom."

Billy left the room, and Carrie took the coffee with her as she wandered around the space she had barely looked at before she fell asleep.

Grace and Billy had installed her in Billy's older brother's room. Evan was in the air force, stationed at an airbase in Saudi Arabia. Grace had explained that he'd gotten emergency leave and was coming back to Seattle, but she wasn't sure when he'd be arriving.

Billy returned from the bathroom and stood watching Carrie from the doorway.

"Billy," Carrie said, examining the plaques, photos, and other framed materials on the walls, "this room is like some kind of military shrine!"

Billy shrugged. "Evan's been in the air force for ten years."

"But it's not just Evan's!" Carrie pointed out. "There's old stuff, too."

Billy walked over to one framed letter and pointed. "This is a letter from President Johnson to my aunt's family in Tacoma," Billy said.

Carrie went over and read it. The letter was dated February 3, 1968, and it expressed the condolences of the President of the United States, Lyndon B. Johnson, at the death by enemy fire in the Mekong Delta of Vietnam of Staff Sergeant Emerson Sampson, First Infantry Division, United States Army.

"Billy, that's horrible," Carrie said quietly. "I didn't know."

"I don't talk about it much," Billy admitted. "I never met my uncle Em. I was born after he died. Dad says he was a great guy."

Carrie was quiet for a moment.

"Everyone in my family served," Billy said, walking over and standing in front of

129

a frame that held several military medals. "My great-grandfather in World War I, my grandfather against the Nazis, my dad in Vietnam, and now Evan."

"But not you," Carrie said thoughtfully.

"Not me," Billy said, his voice a little defiant. "I leave war and the military to other people."

Carrie stood still for a moment, trying to decipher Billy's tone of voice.

"I made my peace with my family's history a long time ago," Billy said, breaking the silence. "Come on, get dressed and meet me downstairs. I'll show you around the house."

Carrie vaguely remembered having stopped in a bathroom the night before, and she found it again. She took the world's fastest shower, pulled on a pair of jeans, a Yale sweatshirt, socks, and tennis shoes, and found Billy downstairs, sitting at the kitchen table, reading the day's Seattle *Post-Intelligencer.*

"Quick change," Billy said. "My dad would approve."

"I'm looking forward to meeting him,"

Carrie said, pulling up a seat near her guy. "Well, actually, I'm a little nervous, too."

"Don't be shocked when you see him," Billy said, offering Carrie a donut from a box on the table. "He doesn't look so great."

Carrie regarded the proferred donut with some distaste, but then figured that Billy's mom hadn't really had a lot of time lately to be thinking about shopping.

"I won't be," Carrie promised, taking a small bite.

"I mean, right now he looks awful. They shaved his head, and there are tubes everywhere." Billy paused. "Also, he's . . . well, he's kind of a hard man," he went on. "You know Kurt's dad?"

Carrie nodded. She'd met Mr. Ackerman more than once, and he was always cantankerous and gruff, even when he was on his best behavior.

"Same type, only military style," Billy said. "And he hates that I play rock and roll."

"He'd like you to be in the army," Carrie suggested.

"Or the navy, or the air force," Billy agreed. "Well, I'm his big disappointment."

"I'm sure he's proud of you," Carrie said.

"I'm not sure he is," Billy said lightly. "But like I said, I made my peace with all that long ago."

"Hey," Carrie said, remembering the night before, "your mother called you Billy James."

Billy smiled again, and took a sip of his own cup of coffee. "You know that's my full name. She's always called me that, and I guess she always will."

Then Carrie remembered something else that Billy had once told her. His mother had always really wanted daughters, and she kept one room in her home decorated like a little girl's room, filled with doilies and antique dolls and a small canopy bed.

"Remember when you told me that there's a girl's room here?" Carrie asked. "Even though you don't have any sisters?"

"Yeah, I remember," Billy said.

I think he was teasing me, Carrie decided. *But I'd better not say that, just in case. I mean, if it's true, it's kind of weird, isn't it?*

"I think . . . I think it sounds kind of

unusual, but you should just tell me if it's true or not," Carrie finally said.

Billy smiled again. "You want to see it?"

Carrie nodded. "Yes, I guess."

Billy took her hand and led her back up the stairs and down the hallway. Two doors past Evan's room was a closed door.

"Open it," Billy instructed.

Carrie did.

The room was perfectly and immaculately decorated. The walls were covered in flowery girlish pink wallpaper. There was a gorgeous canopy bed on which sat several antique dolls, and a fabulous three-story dollhouse took up one corner.

"Wow" was all Carrie could muster.

"The dollhouse is new," Billy commented. "It wasn't here last time I was here."

"Don't you think it's kind of . . . strange?" Carrie asked carefully. "That your mother would do this?"

"Car, all families are strange," Billy replied. "Some are just stranger than others."

Not mine, Carrie thought. *Mine is sickeningly normal.*

"And don't think yours is any exception," Billy joked. "After all, you're from it."

Carrie laughed.

A day doesn't pass that Billy doesn't make me laugh, she thought. She wrapped her arms around him and kissed him. "You're strange, too, you know," she said playfully.

"Sure, I inherited all those weird genes from my mom," Billy joked. He smoothed some hair off her forehead. "Who knows, Car," he said softly. "Maybe one day we'll have a little girl, and she'll fall in love with this room. And then it will all seem perfectly normal, and we'll all say my mom was just psychic about the future or something."

"Maybe so," Carrie agreed softly, smiling up into his eyes.

"C'mon," Billy said, "let's go see my dad."

"How long can we stay?" Billy asked the nurse in the intensive care unit.

"Ten minutes this time," the nurse said. He looked up from the medication cart, where he was checking something off on a list. "Your father's doing better today," he added with a smile.

It was an hour later. Billy and Carrie had taken his father's panel utility van—it read SAMPSON BODY SHOP in big red letters on the side—and crossed the bridge from west Seattle into Seattle proper, then drove past the Kingdome north on the interstate until they got off at the exit for the University of Washington.

Minutes later, they were pulling into the hospital parking garage. And minutes after that they were up in the ICU itself.

Billy led the way through the ICU to the room where his father was. On the way, Carrie had a flashback to when Emma's father had been in the hospital, after his heart attack, in the same kind of intensive care unit.

And when Billy was in the hospital, she recalled with a shudder. *That was the worst night of my life. I love this guy so much. Why was I so hesitant about coming here?*

Billy paused outside his father's room. "This is it," he said to Carrie.

Then he went inside, and Carrie followed. And there, under the beeping heart monitors and blood pressure monitors and blood oxygen regulators, was Mr. Sampson, Billy's dad.

He was asleep, or at least he had his eyes closed.

Billy's right, Carrie thought as she looked at Frank Sampson in some shock. *He does look awful. They shaved his head in order to do the surgery. And there are tubes coming out of his head! Plus there are still casts on both of his legs from his previous accident.* She gulped hard. *Please let me handle this the right way,* she prayed. She glanced quickly over at Billy for reassurance.

"Everything's okay," Billy told her. He walked over to the head of the bed and leaned down. "Dad?" he whispered softly.

Frank Sampson opened his eyes.

"Were you sleeping?" Billy whispered again.

"Heck no," Frank said, his voice hoarse. "Just restin' my eyes."

"Dad," Billy said, "this is Carrie. Carrie Alden."

"Raise the bed a little, son," Mr. Sampson said, indicating the button Billy should push. The head of the bed rose until Frank Sampson was almost sitting up.

"Hello," he said.

"Nice to meet you, sir," Carrie said shyly. "I hope you feel better soon."

"Damn shame for you to see me this way. My boy must think a lot of you, young lady," Frank croaked, "to bring you all this way."

"Carrie came because she wanted to," Billy said, sitting down in a chair near his father's bed.

"Oh," Frank replied. He looked from Billy to Carrie and back again. "Son, can you get me some of that water?"

Billy spotted the water jug on the tray table near his father and poured some in a paper cup. Frank drained it in one gulp.

"Thanks," Frank said. "Got to keep the fluids up, seein' as how they're draining out of me."

Billy smiled, and Carrie managed a small smile, too.

"When can I talk to your doctor?" Billy asked.

"No need," Frank said. "Your mother's doing that."

"I'd like to," Billy said.

"If you want," Frank replied. "When's Evan getting in?"

"I don't know," Billy answered.

"Bring him to see me as soon as he gets here," Frank ordered his son.

"Sure, Dad," Billy answered.

"Right away."

"Okay," Billy said, shifting in his chair a bit. "Is there something you need done? There's nothing Evan can do that I can't do."

Mr. Sampson ignored Billy's comment. "So," he began to Carrie, "what do you think of Billy's old man? I'm a mess, you know. Two broken legs and a shattered pelvis to start with, and then I fall out of bed and bang my head up."

"You'll get better soon," Carrie said encouragingly.

"Shoulda picked a lighter car to have fall on me in the first place," Frank said weakly.

Carrie couldn't help it. She smiled again.

He smiled back at her. "Sense of humor," he said. "Important. Don't lose it."

"I won't," she assured him. She went over to the windowsill and leaned against it.

"I'm just going to close my eyes here for a minute," Mr. Sampson said. "I'm listening to every word you're saying."

A minute later he was snoring.

"Should we leave?" Carrie whispered.

Billy nodded, and they tiptoed out of the room.

"I like your dad," Carrie said when they were back in the corridor. "You know, you look like him."

"Yeah?" Billy asked. "Too bad I didn't turn out like him, though." He put his arm around her shoulders as they walked toward the elevator.

"I think you're a lot like him," Carrie said. "You're both funny, for example."

"That's just about where the similarity ends," Billy said. He pushed the button for the elevator. "It's Evan who's just like Dad, and everyone knows it."

"But Billy—"

"Like I said, Carrie, I know I'm a big disappointment to my father," he said. "It doesn't bother me anymore."

139

Then why do you keep talking about it all the time? Carrie wondered. But she knew she should keep her mouth shut for the moment. So instead of talking, she just put her hand in his and held it tightly, hoping he could feel how much she loved him, and that she wasn't disappointed in him at all.

NINE

"So," Billy asked the next day as he and Carrie sat together by the window of the restaurant in Pike Street Market, "what do you think of Seattle so far?"

Carrie smiled. "It's gorgeous here," she said softly.

"So are you," he said, reaching for her hand across the table.

"Thanks," Carrie said modestly. She'd chosen a long, gauzy white skirt and a white leotard, over which she wore an unstructured beige jacket. She wore beige flats on her feet and a beige straw hat with a white flower. "I don't usually wear light colors."

"I know, you think they make you look fat," Billy said with a chuckle.

"Emma's the only person I know who can wear white all the time and get away with it," Carrie said, taking a sip of her water.

"You're just as pretty as Emma," Billy said. "Prettier."

"Ha," Carrie replied.

"Hey, I happen to be an expert on girls," Billy said with mock severity. "You are beautiful, and curvy, and fantastic. Inside and out."

"I have curvy insides, eh?" Carrie said with a laugh.

Billy pretended to swat at her hand. "You know what I mean."

"Okay," Carrie said. "Anyway, I'm glad you think I'm pretty. And so is Seattle. Really."

"Told you." Billy grinned.

"And it hasn't rained at all!" Carrie marveled. "It's as nice as Sunset Island!"

"Hasn't rained *yet*," Billy corrected, pointing to the umbrella Carrie had by her side. "Remember where you are, Car. People here have umbrellas welded to their bodies."

Carrie and Billy had been back to the hospital several times since their first visit together the day before. Each time Frank seemed the same. He was sleeping a lot, and the doctors weren't sure when they'd be able to move him out of intensive care.

So Billy had taken advantage of one of his father's naps to show Carrie a little bit of Seattle. He took her through the district near the University of Washington, showed her a couple of parks, and then brought her to the flagship Nordstrom's store downtown and bought her a multicolored umbrella.

And now they were having an early dinner at one of the many seafood restaurants in world-famous Pike's Place Market. The host had seated them by one of the windows overlooking Puget Sound, and they had a commanding view of both the sound and the restaurant bar, which was rapidly starting to fill up with a good-looking clientele.

I'm having a great time, Carrie said to herself. *Or at least I would be if Billy's dad weren't so sick and everything weren't so uncertain. And Billy's family is a little . . . well, strange. His mom has that room decorated for a daughter that doesn't exist. And his dad is so gruff all the time. He just keeps asking Billy when his other son is going to get here, as if Billy doesn't matter at all. But I'm glad I'm here. I'm so glad. Mrs. Ricci was right. I love Billy and I have to stick by him.*

And then another voice in her head spoke to her. *For how long?* the voice asked. *What if Billy stays here forever? Are you really going to turn your back on Yale, on all your hopes and dreams? Are you really willing to break your parents' hearts, and throw away your chance to get an education at one of the best schools in the country?*

"You're lost in thought," Billy commented. His words brought Carrie back to the moment.

"A little," she admitted.

"We've got about two hours," Billy said, glancing at his watch. "Then we're due back home."

"You're sure Evan's going to be there?" Carrie asked.

"When it comes to being on time," Billy commented, glancing out the window at the ship traffic on the Sound, "he's always right on the minute."

"I'm looking forward to meeting him, too," Carrie said, taking a sip of the iced tea their waitress had poured for them both.

Billy shook his head.

"He can't be that bad," Carrie began.

"He is," Billy said.

"But—"

"Listen," Billy said, cutting her off. "Some brothers don't get along too well. That's Evan and me. Evan the perfect one and Billy the screw-up."

"You know that isn't true," Carrie said.

"Yeah," Billy agreed. "But my father doesn't."

"Have you tried talking with him?" Carrie asked.

Billy raised his eyebrows. "My father doesn't so much have a conversation as issue orders."

"But if you really tried—"

"Sorry, Car," Billy interrupted. "Every family isn't as reasonable as yours. My dad can be a real sonofabitch to me. He likes you, though."

"I wonder why," Carrie mused.

"The daughter he never had," Billy

145

quipped. He drank some iced tea and glanced around the restaurant. His gaze lingered a moment at the bar before the waitress came up to their table to take their order. Carrie decided on broiled fresh Pacific king salmon, which the waitress said had been caught that very morning, while Billy ordered Alaskan king crab.

The waitress put some fresh bread and fragrant olive oil on their table, and then left them alone again.

"We were talking about your dad," Carrie reminded him.

"Do we have to?" Billy said.

"But . . . I'm confused," Carrie confessed. "I mean, you don't seem to get along with your dad. And yet you're here."

"He's my dad," Billy said.

"I know," Carrie said. "But doesn't that mean you should make more of an effort to really talk to him?"

"I know you want to believe that talking would help, but you just have to take my word for it, it won't."

At that moment someone dropped a glass near the bar area. The crash of breaking glass drew lots of eyes that way, including Billy's and Carrie's.

Suddenly Billy's eyebrows shot up. "Oh, wow," he said under his breath.

Carrie tried to figure out what Billy was looking at. Just then a young woman standing at the bar spotted them, gave a squeal of happy surprise, and then came running down toward them.

She was slender and graceful, about five foot eight, with thick, straight strawberry-blond hair that fell to her shoulders, perfectly proportioned features, and, as Carrie could see as the girl approached, intensely green eyes. She was dressed simply in black leggings and a long green sweater the same color as her eyes.

That girl is gorgeous, Carrie thought. *Absolutely gorgeous.*

"Billy!" she cried. "Billy Sampson!"

"It's Christina," Billy said to Carrie. "I can't believe it."

He got up from his seat and put out his arms, and the girl flew into them. She gave Billy a big embrace, which he returned warmly.

When they finally drew apart, Billy

147

turned to Carrie. "Car," he said, "this is Christina Fitzpatrick. Christina, this is Carrie Alden."

What happened to 'my girlfriend, Carrie Alden'? Carrie thought. *And where have I heard this girl's name before?*

Then it came to her. Christina Fitzpatrick. Billy had told her all about Christina.

She was Billy's old girlfriend, from before he'd met Carrie on Sunset Island the summer before.

Billy always said she was really nice, Carrie recalled. *He never mentioned that she's only the most gorgeous girl I've ever seen. But he did tell me that he had slept with her. . . .*

"Hi," Carrie said, holding her head high. *I will not sound jealous,* she vowed silently. *I will act perfectly normal, as if I meet Billy's drop-dead-gorgeous ex-lovers every day of the week.*

"Pull up a chair," Billy invited eagerly. "Are you here with anyone?"

"Nah," Christina said, "just Susan. Let her wait!" She laughed, a warm, friendly laugh, and Billy joined in merrily. Then she went to the adjoining table, pulled out one of the chairs, and neatly slid it between Carrie and Billy.

And Billy didn't say a word.

"Billy, Billy, Billy," Christina said. "It's so good to see you again."

"Likewise," Billy replied.

"I hear Frank's not doing so good," Christina commented, putting her hand on Billy's.

She called him Frank, Carrie thought, *as if she's known him forever.*

And then another thought hit her.

Maybe she has.

"How'd you find out?" Billy asked her.

"I ran into Grace in the Safeway," Christina replied. "She filled me in. Is he out of the ICU yet?"

"Not yet," Billy said.

Christina's hand was still on Billy's.

"We hope he'll be out soon," Carrie said, wanting to participate in the conversation and at the same time let Christina know that she was there with Billy.

"I'll send something," Christina promised, not taking her eyes off Billy.

"Great," Billy said. He lifted his hand from hers and reached for his iced tea.

"Can I order anything for you, Chris? Food? A drink?"

"No." Christina shook her head. "I'm watching my weight."

"You never had to do that," Billy commented.

Great, Carrie thought. *She's another Sam Bridges, who can eat anything she wants. Unlike his present girlfriend. Okay. I'm through with being reasonable and mature. I officially hate her.*

Christina turned to Carrie, and Carrie felt herself closely scrutinized by those intense green eyes. "So, Carol—"

"It's Carrie," Carrie responded.

Christina smiled. "Sorry," she said. "I'm terrible with names."

"That's okay," Carrie said stiffly. She nervously reached for a piece of the bread, but then pulled her hand away from it.

"So," Christina said, "you and Billy are an item?"

"That's right," Carrie said. She glanced at Billy. He smiled.

"What do you do the rest of the time?" Christina asked, her voice disarmingly friendly.

150

"I'm an au pair on Sunset Island," Carrie replied.

"Is that like some kind of baby-sitter?" Christina asked.

"A little," Carrie admitted. She looked over at Billy for some help.

"Carrie goes to Yale," Billy said, coming to her rescue.

"Yale?" Christina asked. "Ritzy school! I was lucky to get a scholarship to UW. I could never afford Yale."

"Carrie's parents are both pediatricians," Billy supplied.

"Oh, I see," Christina said. "So I guess you can afford Yale."

"They're not rich, if that's what you mean," Carrie said defensively. "They volunteer a lot of time in a free clinic." *And I sound like a total idiot,* she added in her mind.

"I didn't mean to offend you," Christina said quickly.

"No, you didn't," Carrie assured her, since it seemed like the polite thing to say. "So, what are you studying?"

"Bio," Christina replied. "I want to be a vet. And then I want to work right here in Seattle. Isn't it the greatest place?"

"It's nice," Carrie agreed.

"I keep trying to convince Billy to come back, because Seattle's so great for music," Christina related, putting her hand on Billy's again. "I haven't had any luck. So far, anyway."

"Who knows?" Billy offered. "If my father doesn't get better, I may have to come back."

"That would be so great!" Christina exclaimed. "Then we'd all be friends!" She looked at Carrie significantly.

"If Billy comes back to Seattle for good, I'm thinking about coming, too," Carrie said very quickly.

"Oh, you'd hate the rain," Christina replied. "That gets a lot of out-of-towners down about Seattle." She smiled radiantly at Billy. "But for Billy and me, it's home."

Carrie looked out the window for a moment, and all she could see was sunlight glinting off the water.

"Hi, Jane," Carrie said into the phone as she sat back on Evan's bed. "Is Emma there?"

"Oh, hi, Carrie!" Jane Hewitt said. "Hold on a second, she's upstairs."

It was two hours after Billy and Carrie had gotten back to the Sampsons' house. Evan was expected to arrive at any minute, and Carrie had decided to take a few minutes and check in with Emma back on Sunset Island.

I'm still not recovered from dinner, Carrie thought. *It's totally obvious to me that Christina would love to get Billy back if she could! He claimed I was imagining things. And he swore up and down he isn't interested in her anymore. I wonder how long that would last if he was here and I was far, far away.*

"Hi, Carrie," Emma's familiar voice came on the phone.

"Hi, Emma," Carrie said. "How are things on the island?"

"Never mind the island," Emma said. "How are you? How's Billy's dad?"

"He'll be okay," Carrie replied, pulling her knees up to her chest. "And I'm okay."

"You don't sound okay," Emma noted.

"No, I'm all right," Carrie said. "Seattle is very pretty."

"Carrie, I know you too well," Emma said. "Something is wrong. Is it Billy's dad?"

"No, he's doing pretty well."

"What, then?"

Carrie sighed and stretched out on the bed. "Did you ever feel like your first name should be Dogmeat?"

"What?"

"Wait, scratch that," Carrie corrected herself. "You're tiny and gorgeous. I'll bet you never have a day when you feel like the Goodyear blimp."

"Carrie, what are you talking about?" Emma asked, concern in her voice.

"Oh nothing," Carrie said lightly. "Just that I met Billy's old girlfriend today."

"You're joking," Emma said flatly.

"No joke," Carrie answered. "And compared to her, I look like ten miles of bad road, as Pres would say."

"I'm sure that's not true," Emma said quickly.

"Trust me, Em," Carrie said with a dry laugh. "I'm not exaggerating. She is walking perfection."

154

"Carrie, you know Billy's totally committed to you," Emma said.

"I know," Carrie replied with a sigh. "I know I shouldn't make comparisons. And I know Billy thinks I'm beautiful. And I tell myself that I'm smart and nice and blah, blah, blah. But I still end up feeling like the before photo in a diet ad."

"You know that's in your head," Emma said firmly.

"I know that I'm acting like an insecure idiot, that's what I know," Carrie said.

"He asked you to go to Seattle with him, didn't he?" Emma reminded her.

"Yes," Carrie answered, "but . . ."

"But what?"

"This girl, Christina, she'd go after him again if she could," Carrie said. "I just know it!"

"How can you know that?" Emma queried.

"She made it perfectly obvious," Carrie said. "I don't need to be psychic to figure this one out."

"Did you talk about it with Billy?" Emma asked.

"A little," Carrie admitted.

155

"What did he say?" Emma asked.

Carrie shifted the phone from her left ear to her right ear. "He said I was out of my mind, and that he loved only me."

"Do you believe him?" Emma asked slowly.

"I guess," Carrie said dubiously.

"Did he see her last time he was there?" Emma asked. "Earlier this summer?"

"No," Carrie answered. "I don't think so."

"See?" Emma asked. "You're getting all worked up over nothing."

"I don't know, Emma," Carrie said. "I've got the weirdest feeling about all this."

"How so?"

"Like if I left Seattle and Billy had to stay," Carrie said slowly, "I'd lose Billy to her."

"That doesn't make any sense," Emma said.

"Maybe not," Carrie said. "But it's how I feel." *And it's pretty much what Mrs. Ricci told me, too,* she added in her mind. *She said I had to be careful not to lose Billy. Maybe what she meant was that I'd have to stay in Seattle!*

"This reminds me of that dream you

had," Emma said thoughtfully. "You know, that nightmare."

Carrie recalled that she'd once told Emma about a bad dream she'd had in which Billy was in love with another girl. *And he invited me to his wedding with her!* she remembered.

"But that was just a dream," Emma reminded her. "It was all just in your head."

"I know," Carrie said ruefully. "But this is real."

"Carrie," Emma said, "let me tell you what you'd tell me."

"Go ahead," Carrie said dully.

"You'd say," Emma continued, "that you're not looking at things realistically."

"I would?"

"You'd say that since Billy and Christina—that's her name?"

"Yes," Carrie answered.

"That since Billy and Christina have known each other for so long, of course they'd be friendly to each other."

"Well, yeah," Carrie said.

"It's like you and Josh, Carrie," Emma said. "If you ran into him, you'd be friendly, right?"

"Right," Carrie answered truthfully. "But this wasn't like that."

"Maybe it was."

"No," Carrie insisted. "I just know it, right in my gut." She put her hand on her stomach. "I could lose him, Emma. I know I could."

For another twenty minutes Emma tried to convince Carrie that her feelings didn't make any sense. But try as she might, Carrie couldn't shake the idea that if she went back to Sunset Island the day after next and left Billy in Seattle, she might never see him again.

TEN

One more day, Carrie thought as she adjusted the pillow under her head. *One more day.*

I have to decide by tomorrow what I'm going to do if Billy tells me he's going to stay. Which is exactly what I think he's going to tell me.

It was very early the next morning, and Carrie had awakened before anyone else in the Sampson house. Billy was asleep in his room. His older brother, Evan, who had arrived the previous night at about nine o'clock, dressed in his air force uniform, was sleeping on the couch in the family room downstairs.

And I don't know what to do, Carrie thought as she lay in bed, staring at the

159

ceiling. *I have no idea whether to stay or go. I wish Mrs. Ricci were here to help me!*

"You're losing it, Carrie," she mumbled to herself. "You think a psychic can figure your problems out for you."

She sat up and sighed. *Okay, I just have to put it out of my mind for a little while,* she told herself, *or I'm going to make myself totally crazy.*

She grabbed an old copy of *Rock On!* that had somehow been stashed in the nightstand next to Evan's bed, determined to temporarily take her mind off her crisis. She started leafing through it, and a bold, four-color advertisement in the back caught her eye.

PSYCHIC 900 BUDDIES HOTLINE! Got a problem you can't figure out? Call the Psychic 900 Buddies Hotline and get the advice of a professional, *certified* psychic. No problem too big or too small. Just $1.99 a minute, and the first three minutes are free to first-time callers! You will want to call again and again. Call now!

"Oh, no," Carrie said out loud. "I'm not that big a sucker." She put down the magazine. Then she picked it up again.

I know about 900 numbers. A lot of times they're a total rip-off. But this might be different. . . . No, it isn't different. It's a rip-off. But what if someone like Mrs. Ricci answers the phone? It might help! And the first three minutes are free.

If it looks like it's not going to be of any use, I'll just hang up before they start billing me.

Quietly Carrie got out of bed, made sure the door was closed, and picked up the cordless phone that she'd left in the bedroom after her call to Emma the evening before. Then she got her small travel alarm clock and set it to tell her when three minutes had passed.

"It's a good thing Sam doesn't know I'm doing this," Carrie said with a sigh, looking at the magazine ad again. "I'd never live it down."

She tiptoed to the door once more to make sure no one could overhear her, then tiptoed back to the bed, picked up the phone, and dialed.

Someone answered on the second ring.

"Psychic 900 Buddies Hotline!" a female voice chirped. "We're glad you called!"

"My name is Carrie," Carrie said very quietly.

"Pardon me?" the voice said loudly. "I can't hear you!"

Carrie winced. To her it sounded as if the voice was booming throughout the house. "I said my name is Carrie," she repeated a little more clearly. "And I'd like a psychic consultation."

"Well, Carrie, you've done the right thing by calling us!" the voice assured her. "Love, work, or money?"

"What?" Carrie asked.

"You're definitely a first-time caller!" the woman said gaily. "Otherwise you'd know the drill. Know how I knew that?"

"No," Carrie said.

"I'm psychic!" the woman chortled. "Okay, you want a first consultation with a love psychic, a work psychic, or a money psychic?"

Carrie thought a moment. "You mean there are specialities?"

"Uh-huh," the psychic said. "We're the

only psychic hotline with experts in specific fields," she bragged.

"Gee, kind of like doctors," Carrie said with a faint smile.

"Yes, well, we think of ourselves as spiritual doctors to the universe," the voice said proudly. "Now, which type of psychic buddy did you want?"

"Love," Carrie admitted.

"One love psychic coming right up!" the woman said. "Know how I know that?"

"You're psychic?" Carrie replied, closing her eyes wearily.

"Nope," the woman chirped, "I'm the operator! Hold on!"

Carrie heard a series of beeps, and then another woman's voice came on the line.

"This is Lady Letitia," the voice said. "May I help you?"

"My name's Carrie," Carrie said, "and I'm looking for some advice." She glanced at the clock. Only two minutes and thirty seconds left until she would start to be billed for the call.

"Well," the psychic said, "tell me your love problem, and I'll give you the answer. Lady Letitia has never failed."

Quickly Carrie outlined for Lady Letitia the situation with Billy, Billy's father, and why she was in Seattle.

"And one more thing," Carrie concluded. "His brother, who's in the air force, came in last night."

"Uh-huh, uh-huh," Lady Letitia said. "Well, let me tell you what vibes I'm getting on this."

Brrring! The alarm clock went off. The free three minutes were up.

I'll talk fast, Carrie decided. *I can't just hang up now.*

"My vibes tell me that the brother can solve your problem for you," Lady Letitia said.

Carrie sighed. "Not really," she said. "He said his enlistment will be up soon, so if he had to, he could stay here and help his dad and mom, instead of Billy doing it. But what he really wants to do is reenlist!"

"Maybe he and your guy should talk things over," Lady Letitia suggested.

"They hate each other," Carrie said matter-of-factly. "They don't talk."

"That's too bad," Lady Letitia offered unhelpfully.

"No one in the whole family really seems to talk to anyone else," Carrie said morosely. "It's driving me crazy!"

"Uh-huh, uh-huh," Lady Letitia agreed. "I can see how that could be a problem."

"I mean, how can you work anything out if you can't communicate?" Carrie cried.

"So true," the psychic agreed.

"The only things Billy's dad ever says to him are negative," Carrie continued.

"That's a shame," Lady Letitia sympathized.

"I know!" Carrie agreed. "He thinks what Billy does with his music is stupid!"

"I see."

"So does his brother, Evan," Carrie said. "But everyone isn't cut out to be in the military, you know?"

"I do," Lady Letitia agreed.

"And Billy has so much talent!" Carrie went on. "It would be a sin if he turned his back on that kind of gift, that's what I think! Why can't his family support his choice? Why do they keep trying to make him into what they want him to be, instead of accepting him for who he really is?"

"I see troubled waters," Lady Letitia said.

"Of course you do!" Carrie exclaimed. "This whole situation is troubled waters! I love Billy, and I want to be with him forever. But what am I supposed to do if he stays here because he feels guilty? Am I supposed to just give up Yale? My parents would kill me! And not only that, I feel like I'd be throwing away all my dreams! I've worked so hard already to get recognized as a photographer for the newspaper there—not many freshman photographers get any kind of recognition at all, you know?"

"Uh-huh, uh-huh," the psychic murmured.

"But I did it!" Carrie cried. "I worked my butt off! And I have all these dreams. I wouldn't expect Billy to give up his dreams for me!"

"Right," Lady Letitia agreed.

"On the other hand, he's not really asking me to give up my dreams, I guess," Carrie went on. "Going to a different college isn't giving up my dreams, is it? And if I'm not here, isn't that telling him that I

166

don't really support him, just like his parents? And what about Christina? You can't tell me she isn't dying to get back together with him!"

"Uh-huh, uh-huh," Lady Letitia uttered.

"And then there's—" All of a sudden Carrie realized she was ranting on and on about her life to some voice on the phone. And not only that, she was paying by the minute.

I've totally lost my mind, she told herself. *I'd better cut to the psychic chase here.*

"So please tell me what you think," Carrie said quickly. "And please do it fast."

"Well," Lady Letitia said, "your phone vibes tell me that you have to do what you have to do."

"I have to do what I have to do?" Carrie echoed incredulously.

"Deep in your spiritual center, you know the truth," Lady Letitia said mysteriously. "My job is only to bring out that truth, bring it to your consciousness."

"Great," Carrie said. "Do it. But I can only afford one more minute."

"I'm sorry," the psychic said regretfully. "It will take longer than a minute to get to the heart of it. But don't you think spiritual peace of mind is worth it?"

"Well, I—"

"I hold the answers right here," Lady Letitia said. "What is money without peace of mind?"

"What is peace of mind without money?" Carrie shot back. "Sorry," she added, and then she quickly hung up the phone.

"Carrie Alden," she told herself, leaning back on the bed, "you are the world's biggest fool. And now you're going to have to explain to Billy's parents about the little phone call you just put on their phone bill!"

"I've made my decision," Billy said as he and Carrie walked along the Puget Sound shoreline.

Carrie took a sharp breath.

I can handle it, she told herself. *Whatever it is, I can handle it.*

"I'm going to stay here," Billy said. "My family needs me."

She gulped hard. "Are you sure?" she asked him.

"My father's not going to be well enough to work anytime soon," Billy said. "Things

168

are going to hell in a handbasket at his shop. I've got to stay."

Carrie took her boyfriend by the arm. "But what about the band?" she asked softly. "What about everything back on the island?"

"It'll have to wait," Billy replied philosophically. "Let's stop here for a minute." He sat down on the rocky beach, and Carrie sat down next to him. It was another glorious day, and the sun sparkled off the sound.

"Look, Carrie," Billy said, turning to her. "This isn't easy for me."

"I know," Carrie said softly.

"I just . . . every choice I could make feels like the wrong thing to do," Billy said.

"I just don't think it's fair," Carrie said, trying to be reasonable and measured but feeling tears well up in her eyes. "Your band is about to get a recording contract!"

"Maybe," Billy said, averting his eyes. "And maybe not."

"If you're not there, it won't happen," Carrie said.

"Don't you think I know that?" Billy said sharply. "But my family has to come first."

"Even though they criticize you and put you down?" Carrie said.

Billy stared at her. "If you were in my position, what would you do?"

Carrie didn't reply.

"I think Polimar will wait," Billy said, as if he was trying to talk himself into it. "If they want to sign us, they'll wait."

Carrie stared out into the distance for a minute. "But it's not as if your older brother can't stay instead of you," she finally said.

"Evan doesn't want to," Billy replied. "That's his decision."

"But your parents would rather have him stay instead of you!" Carrie cried. "You think so yourself!"

"No," he said bitterly. "My mom told me last night that my brother is actually 'making something of his life.' Unlike you-know-who."

"But Billy, don't you see?" Carrie cried, turning to him. "You're trying to make it up to your parents for not going into the military or something. You want to stay because you feel guilty! It's as if . . . as if you think you can finally be their perfect little boy if you do this now!"

"That's bull."

"No, it isn't!" Carrie insisted. "I could understand if you didn't have a brother. But why should Evan's plans be more important than yours?"

Billy didn't answer.

"That is just so unfair!" Carrie cried. "Why can't *his* plans wait?"

"Well, it won't be forever," Billy replied, his voice still bitter.

"Won't it?" Carrie whispered. "What if you don't get to come back to the island at all? Are you just going to give up the Flirts?"

Tears formed in Billy's eyes. "There are bands in Seattle. Or I'll put together another one. Or maybe I'll get Pres to come live out here, too."

"It just isn't fair," Carrie repeated.

"Life's not fair," Billy pointed out, gruffly brushing his tears away. Then he turned to her and looked deeply into Carrie's eyes.

I know what he's waiting for, Carrie thought. *He's waiting to see what I say about moving out here to be with him. Forever.*

"So?" Billy asked.

"I'm not sure," Carrie answered honestly.

"Carrie—"

"Yes," Carrie cried, "I know, I have to decide!"

"It's not so hard," Billy said gently. "I've got it all worked out."

"You do?" Carrie asked.

"It'll be just like I said on the island," Billy murmured, taking Carrie's hand. "We'll get a little place down here on the Sound—it's beautiful, don't you think? You can go to the U—they've got a great newspaper there, too."

"I can't transfer now," Carrie replied.

"So what's a semester?" Billy asked her. "In the big picture, it doesn't amount to anything! Just work for a semester."

"Doing what?" Carrie asked.

"Whatever people do!" Billy exploded. "People get jobs all the time. You'll get a job!"

"What about my family?" Carrie said. "And the Templetons?"

"Jeez, Carrie, they'll understand!" Billy said, tightening his grip on her hand. "They're grown-ups. *You're* a grown-up."

Carrie was silent. All the advice she'd gotten from Mrs. Ricci and Emma didn't seem to amount to anything now.

I'm going to have to make this decision on my own, she thought. *No one's going to be able to tell me what to do.*

"What happens if I can't come?" Carrie asked quietly, looking at Billy.

Billy looked as though someone had slapped him in the face. "You mean won't," he said in a low voice.

"I'm not saying that's my decision," Carrie added quickly. "I'm just asking, what if?"

Billy exhaled slowly. "I don't know, Car. I'd be seriously bummed."

Carrie looked out over the Sound. Ferryboats were heading to and from Bainbridge Island, the sun was glinting off the skyscrapers of downtown Seattle—everywhere, life was normal.

He said he'd be bummed. He didn't say he'd stand by me forever, she thought.

"You know about long-distance relationships," Billy continued. "We'd try, but . . ." His voice trailed off.

173

Carrie turned to him. "Billy," she said, "I'm not sure yet."

"You may never be sure," he said. "But you're gonna have to make a choice anyway."

"Yeah," Carrie said faintly.

"I know what I'm asking isn't easy," Billy continued. "But if you really believe in us . . ."

Carrie looked at him sharply. "Would you do it for me?"

"What do you mean?"

"I mean what if everything was great with the Flirts, and I needed to go back to New Jersey for my family? Would you give up the band to follow me? And start a new band in New Jersey?"

"That's not the same thing—"

"Yes, it is," Carrie maintained. "Asking me to give up Yale to go to another college is just like my asking you to give up the Flirts to form another band."

"I don't think it *is* the same thing, Car," Billy said sincerely. "But I'll tell you this. I love you. I want to spend my life with you. And if we're not together . . . it would break my heart."

Now tears came to Carrie's eyes, and she wrapped her arms around Billy's shoulders. "I love you, too, Billy," she whispered. "So much." She kissed him softly, then buried her head in his shoulder. "I'll decide by tomorrow, okay?"

He nodded, pulling her even closer.

Carrie closed her eyes and reveled in the feel and the smell of the guy she loved. But her heart was torn into pieces, and she had absolutely no idea what to do about it.

ELEVEN

Today I have to make the decision that will alter the entire course of my life.

That's the first thing Carrie thought when her eyes sprang open the next morning. She glanced at the alarm clock. Six-thirty. Carrie slumped back on the bed, as depressed and anxious as she'd ever felt in her life.

My flight back to Maine is at one this afternoon, Carrie thought. *That is, unless I change it. Or cancel it completely.*

Mrs. Ricci can't help me now. No one can help me.

Before she went to sleep the night before, Carrie had tried to attack her problem logically. She'd actually torn out a sheet of paper from an old notebook she found in the room and made a list on it with the green pen she'd found in the nightstand.

Now Carrie picked it up and stared at it, as if it might give her a message from the great beyond.

TO STAY OR TO GO

Reasons to stay	*Reasons to go*
I love Billy	Yale and my career
Christina: she might move in on him	Commitment to the Templetons
My future with Billy	Commitment to my parents
Support Billy	My future
Help Billy's family	Don't want to uproot my life totally
	Gut instinct says go

Carrie stared at the piece of paper

Every reason to stay has to do with Billy, she suddenly realized.

Then Carrie inhaled sharply. She had an idea—maybe it was even a good one.

Why didn't I think of this before? she asked herself. But she knew why. *It's because I've been looking to someone else— psychics—to solve this problem, instead of really looking inside myself.*

I just hope there's still time, Carrie thought, getting out of bed and dressing quickly.

As she dressed, her plan continued to form.

And the time to put it into action, Carrie thought, *is right now.*

"Evan?" Carrie said softly as she stood next to the family-room couch where Billy's older brother was sleeping.

"Mmmmrph?" Evan mumbled, still asleep.

"Evan?" Carrie asked again.

"Huh?" Evan opened his eyes. They widened in surprise when he saw that it was Carrie who was saying his name, particularly because he and Carrie hadn't exchanged more than three or four sentences since he'd come home from Saudi Arabia.

"I made coffee," Carrie said. "Do you want some?"

"Yeah," Evan mumbled. "But why'd you wake me? Is my dad all right?"

"He's fine," Carrie assured him. "I want to talk to you."

"Me?" Evan asked skeptically.

"Yes," Carrie said softly.

Evan shrugged. "Fine," he said. "I'll meet you in the kitchen in five minutes."

Carrie went into the kitchen to wait. She could hear Evan get out of bed and go into the downstairs bathroom. In exactly five minutes he came into the kitchen dressed in a pair of jeans and an old flannel shirt.

He looks just like an older version of Billy, Carrie thought for about the fiftieth time since she'd met him. *That's what Billy would look like with a military haircut.*

She began to get nervous. *What am I, an eighteen-year-old girl, going to say to this twenty-eight-year-old man who's spent the last ten years in the armed forces? Who am I kidding?*

Evan sat down at the table and looked up at Carrie with the same brown eyes that Billy had.

"So," he said flatly. "What can I do for you?"

Carrie sat across from him. "I wanted to talk to you about Billy," she said hesitantly. "And about me."

"I don't know what there is to talk about," Evan said, sipping his coffee.

"No one in your family seems to talk very much," Carrie said. "I've noticed that."

Evan shrugged but didn't say a word.

"I . . . it's kind of hard for me," Carrie continued. "I mean, my family talks a lot."

Evan shrugged again. "Different styles suit different people."

"Right," Carrie agreed, nervously turning her coffee cup around in her hands. "But I thought . . . I just thought that maybe I could talk to you."

Evan sipped his coffee again. "I'm listening," he said.

"Good," Carrie managed. She took a deep breath. "I guess you don't know much about me."

"Just what my mom's written to me,"

Evan replied. "That you're from New Jersey and you're going to Yale." The words were clipped.

Ouch, Carrie thought. *This guy sounds so defensive, so closed emotionally. This isn't going to be easy. In fact, it's probably not even going to work.*

"Well," Carrie said, pressing on, "maybe you should try to find out for yourself."

"Why?" Evan asked, taking another sip of his coffee. "What's the point?"

"Because I might be a member of your family someday," Carrie said, feeling she had nothing to lose. "It's the same reason I'm interested in your uncle Emerson."

Carrie saw a momentary look of interest cross Evan's face.

"Army Staff Sergeant Emerson Sampson," Carrie recited. "Killed in action in the Mekong Delta in 1968."

Evan was looking at her closely now. "Let me show you something," he said. "Wait here." He got up and left the room.

What's this about? Carrie thought, confused.

Evan came back into the kitchen holding his wallet. He slowly opened it to the section where his family pictures were and extracted one of the photos. He put it on the table.

It was a somewhat faded photo of a man dressed in Army fatigues, holding a little boy in his arms.

"That's Uncle Emerson," Evan said. "And that's me he's holding. Billy wasn't even born yet."

"You must be very proud of him," Carrie said softly, picking up the photo and holding it.

"Family. Proud of my family," Evan said tersely.

"You're not proud of Billy," Carrie pointed out. "Not at all."

"Why should I be?" Evan asked, his voice getting a little hot. "He lets everyone down."

That's not true! Carrie wanted to cry, but she bit back her retort. "He told me he's staying here in Seattle," she said quietly.

Evan stared into his coffee. "He probably feels guilty," he surmised.

"Maybe," Carrie agreed. "But not because he did anything wrong. He loves all of you and he wants you all to be proud of him, and he feels that it's his fault you *aren't* proud of him."

"Then all he has to do is lead his life the right way," Evan said succinctly.

Carrie thought for a moment. "What if . . . what if everyone in your family was a musician, and everyone expected you and Billy to be musicians, too? And Billy had all this musical talent, so the family was so proud of him. But you weren't born with any musical talent, and so you decided to go into the military, which is what you were good at."

Evan narrowed his eyes at Carrie. "It's not the same thing. Anyone—anyone honorable—can choose military service."

"Billy's honorable," Carrie said. "He just doesn't have the same calling as you do."

"He could if he wanted to," Evan said stubbornly. "But like I said, he lets everyone down."

"He doesn't let me down," Carrie said softly.

"You're not family," Evan pointed out.

"Well," Carrie said, choosing her words very carefully, "when your dad had his accident, who was the one who came back?"

Evan was silent.

"Billy," he finally said.

"He cares!" Carrie cried. Then she lowered her voice so it wouldn't carry through the house. "He really does care, Evan."

"Good," Evan said, getting up from the table. "Now he can prove it."

Carrie made no move to get up.

"Do you understand what it would mean for him to stay here?" Carrie asked. "In terms of his career, I mean?"

"What career?" Evan said derisively. "He acts like he's fifteen, playing in some garage band so he can get girls!"

"That's not why he does it," Carrie said in a level voice. "Billy is really, truly gifted, Evan. I'm telling you the truth. He and his band have come so far—they're about to get a recording contract with a major label. But it won't happen if Billy leaves Sunset Island."

"That's all very well and good, but why are *you* telling me this?" Evan said, sitting back down. "If Billy has something to say to me, he can say it himself."

"No, he can't," Carrie pointed out. "No more than you can talk to him."

Evan was silent once again. "You've got a point," he finally admitted.

Carrie filled him in on the details of the upcoming Flirts tour, and about how Polimar Records was going to make their final decision on the band.

"If he stays here," Carrie said, "he can't do that."

"Please," Evan said derisively. "You think rock and roll is a career, Carrie?"

"Yes!" Carrie exclaimed. "It is for Billy! Don't you see? Everyone has to choose their own destiny, Evan!"

"Carrie, you seem like a nice girl," Evan said. "But that is some kind of New Age hogwash. Sometimes you have to do what's *right*. Maybe you're too young to understand that yet."

"I'm not too young to know about duty and honor," Carrie said in a level voice. "And I still believe that every person has to choose their own path in life. Nothing you can say will change my mind."

Evan just shrugged.

I'm losing ground, Carrie thought desperately. *Okay, it's now or never. Pres told Sam once that if you've got an ace in the hole, it doesn't do you any good unless you play it. It's time to play my ace.*

"You listen to rock," Carrie said slowly. "I know you do. You were talking about it yesterday."

"And?" Evan challenged.

"And I bet you've never even listened to Billy's music," Carrie said.

"That's not true!" Evan replied. Angrily he shoved his coffee cup away.

"When?" Carrie asked.

"When he was a kid," Evan admitted.

"He's not a kid anymore," Carrie said.

Evan reached over, took a tangerine out of the fruit bowl on the table, and started to peel it. Carrie waited.

"No," Evan finally admitted. "He isn't."

Carrie reached into the back pocket of her pants and took out a cassette tape. It was the demo tape that Billy and Pres had recently done in the studio in Portland. Emma and Sam weren't on it—it was just Pres, Billy, Jay Bailey on keyboards, and Jake Fisher on drums.

She put the cassette tape on the table.

"Get your Walkman?" Carrie asked.

"I'm not going to—"

"Please?" Carrie asked.

Evan stared at the tape, then back at Carrie. "Okay," he said, "but don't think this is going to change my mind."

"Just listen to it," Carrie said.

Evan went into the living room to get his Walkman. He came back to the kitchen and handed it to Carrie. She popped in the cassette tape and gave it back to him.

"What am I listening to?" Evan asked irritably.

"Just listen," Carrie said.

Skeptically Evan picked up the head-phones and put them to his ears. He reached down and pressed the play button, sat back in his chair, and began to listen.

He listened for three minutes. Carrie expected him to snap the Walkman off then, after the first song.

But Evan didn't. He listened to the second song. Five minutes into the tape, he closed his eyes.

And he kept them closed until the four-song demo tape was finished, ten minutes later.

Then he opened his eyes.

"He's good," Evan conceded. "Damn good."

Carrie smiled.

"No, I'm serious," Evan said. "The kid is really, really good. The second song there—what is it called, 'Love Junkie' or something?—I loved that."

"Evan," Carrie said, leaning toward him, all the conviction of her heart in her voice, "this is Billy's chance. Sometimes you only get one chance."

Evan sat thoughtfully for a moment.

"You said he's going on tour in a couple of weeks?" Evan asked.

Carrie nodded.

"And that Polimar's going to decide right away?" Evan queried.

Carrie nodded again.

Oh, please, she prayed. *Please let Evan see how talented Billy is. Please.*

Evan stood up and paced the kitchen. Then he stopped and stared out the window. "You know, I don't remember Uncle Em. He died when I was only a year old. But I saw a letter he wrote to my dad from Vietnam when I was born. I must have read that letter a hundred times. He wrote, 'Frank, it's a big world out there. Make sure your son makes something out of his life. Don't let him waste God's gifts. Help him—let him—be all he can be.'" He continued to stare out the window for a moment. Then, finally, he turned back to Carrie.

"I'm not gonna let Billy say I stood in his way," Evan said.

"Oh, thank you!" Carrie cried, jumping up.

"Hold on," Evan cautioned, holding up his hand. "Let's get a few ground rules straight."

Carrie nodded and waited expectantly.

"I'll get a hardship leave from the Air Force and stay here for a while. And I'll put off my reenlistment. Not forever, mind you, but for a few months," Evan continued.

Carrie felt a surge of relief wash over her.

"Oh, thank you!" she murmured, her hands over her heart.

"Hey," Evan warned, "I said for a few months. To see what happens. Not forever."

"Evan," Carrie said fervently, "I can't thank you enough."

Just then Billy walked into the kitchen wearing an old, ratty bathrobe. Carrie could see how surprised he was to see her and Evan sitting at the table together.

"I just saved your butt, little brother," Evan said gruffly.

"What?" Billy asked.

Carrie ran over to Billy and threw herself into his arms. "Oh, I love you, I love you!" she cried. "And I love Evan! I love everybody!"

"What are you talking about?" Billy asked, totally confused.

"Billy," Carrie said, her eyes shining with tears of happiness, "it's okay now. It's all going to be okay. We can go home. We can go home!"

TWELVE

"Hey, Car, maybe the Flirts will want to do one of my tunes!" Ian suggested as Carrie pulled the car into the driveway of the Flirts' house. Evidently while Carrie had been away in Seattle, Ian and Becky had gotten back together.

"Yeah," Becky agreed from the backseat. "Ian is a genius, you know."

It was two days later, and Carrie and Billy were back on the island. Carrie, Ian, and Becky were headed to the Flirts's band practice. Billy had invited Ian to sit in on the rehearsal, and Ian had asked if he could bring Becky, who was already over at the Templetons' house.

"Well, you know the Flirts write all their

own stuff," Carrie reminded Ian as she put the car in park.

"I know," Ian agreed. "But even Billy Joel occasionally covers someone else's stuff, if it's really great."

"And Ian is a genius," Becky said again, getting out of the car.

Carrie laughed. "I'm glad to see you two made up."

Ian grinned and put his arm around Becky, who was slightly taller than he was. "It was just a misunderstanding, right?"

"Right," Becky agreed. "Hey, did you know Ian wrote a song about me?"

And it wasn't very complimentary, Carrie recalled. *All about how cold you are and how you broke his heart and didn't care.*

"Yeah, I heard the song," Carrie said carefully. She knocked on the front door of Billy's house.

"Well, isn't it incredible?" Becky cried. "I mean, I could go down in rock history with, like, all the cool girls cool guys have written songs about, you know?"

"Sure," Carrie agreed.

"You really are a genius," Becky told Ian again. He kissed her passionately, and

Carrie looked everywhere except at the two of them.

"Hey, girlfriend!" Sam cried, pulling open the door. She gave Carrie a quick hug. "I am so glad you guys are back!"

Carrie hugged Sam. She hadn't had a chance to see either Sam or Emma since her return, since Claudia was keeping her so busy with the kids. But she had called them both and explained in detail what had happened in Seattle.

"It's good to be home," Carrie agreed.

"You pulled off, like, this major coup!" Sam exclaimed. "You're amazing!"

Carrie gestured at Ian and Becky, who were still kissing. "I may be amazing, but Ian is a genius," Carrie said with a laugh.

Sam took in the sight of Ian and Becky. "Ah, young love," she quipped. She tapped Becky on the shoulder. "Uh, Becky? Do you think you could come up for air?"

Becky and Ian pulled apart. "What?" Becky said. "Oh, yeah, sure."

Everyone walked into the living room, where the band had already set up for rehearsal. Emma and Erin were adjusting

195

their mikes. When they saw Carrie, they both ran over to her and hugged her.

"Boy, are we happy to see you," Erin said with a grin.

"Thanks," Carrie said.

"We were already figuring out a plan to kidnap you and Billy and drag you both back here," Emma said, squeezing Carrie's hand.

Carrie looked around. "Where's Billy?"

"He's upstairs on the phone with Evan," Emma explained.

Carrie looked worried. "Is everything okay?"

"Everything's fine," Sam assured her. "Billy just called in for a progress report. So what's Billy's brother like?"

"He's . . . different from Billy," Carrie allowed. "But a good guy, underneath all that military stuff."

"You know I love guys in uniform," Sam said, wiggling her eyebrows.

"Sure," Erin agreed. "In uniform, out of uniform, any way you can get them!"

"You teasin' my lady?" Pres drawled, loping over to them. He gave Carrie a warm hug. "Hey, girl."

Carrie hugged him back. "It's so good to see you. I feel like I've been away forever instead of for a few days."

"Billy told me what you did," Pres said with admiration, his arms still around Carrie. "You are something else."

"I didn't really do that much," Carrie said.

"Yeah, you did," Pres said. "If it hadn't been for you, Billy would be back in Seattle and the Flirts might be history."

"I'm just really glad it worked out," Carrie said.

"So ol' Evan is going to hang out in Seattle for a few months and give us our shot," Pres said. "Right?"

Carrie nodded. "That's what he agreed to."

"I know we're getting a deal with Polimar this time," Sam said with conviction. "Nothing can stop us!"

"Not even Diana De Witt!" Jay Bailey said, crossing the room. Jake Fisher was beside him.

"Hey, do we get to add our thanks?" Jake asked, giving Carrie a friendly pat on the shoulder.

"You guys, I don't feel like I deserve all this credit," Carrie began.

"You do," Jay insisted. "Billy told us everything."

"How did you figure out that you should talk to Evan yourself?" Emma asked.

"And play him some of the Flirts' tunes?" Erin added. "That was brilliant!"

"Let's just say I was desperate," Carrie said with a laugh. She looked around the room. "Hey, where did Ian and Becky go?"

Everyone turned around.

"I don't know," Emma said. "They were here a minute ago."

"I'll go look," Sam said with a sigh. "Becky probably has Ian tied up somewhere."

"No, I'll go," Carrie said. "Excuse me." She checked the rest of the downstairs, but found no one. Quickly she went upstairs. Both the door to Billy's room and the door to Pres's room were closed. She stood outside Billy's door and listened. She could hear his voice.

"So you'll call me if there's any change?" he was saying. "Yeah . . . yeah. Listen, Evan, thanks. I mean it." More silence. "I'll try," Billy said in a husky voice, and then he said good-bye.

Carrie knocked softly on the door.

"Yeah?"

She opened the door. "Hi."

Billy grinned at her. "Hi." He held out his arms to her.

She crossed the room and was instantly in Billy's arms. "I heard the end of your conversation," she admitted. "I hope that was okay."

"Sure," Billy said, his voice muffled by Carrie's hair. "I can't believe Evan changed his mind. I mean, I'm here, and I know it's true, but I still can't believe it."

"He loved your music," Carrie said. "That's what did it."

Billy held Carrie at arm's length and gazed into her eyes. "It's more than that, Car," he said. "You did it. For me."

"For us," she said simply.

Billy nodded. "For us."

"And all I did was talk to him," Carrie pointed out. "If he hadn't been impressed by your music, you'd still be in Seattle."

"He never wanted to listen before."

"I know," Carrie said quietly.

"He told me he took a tape to the hospital and played it for Dad," Billy said with wonder. "And Dad actually listened!"

"That's wonderful, Billy!"

Billy pulled Carrie close again. "You know what else Evan said? He told me to go out there and make something out of my life. He said I shouldn't waste God's gifts, that I should be all I can be."

Carrie smiled. *That's exactly what Evan and Billy's uncle wrote to Frank when Evan was born,* Carrie realized. *Billy was born after his uncle died, but I guess he ended up getting the message as well.*

"That's wonderful, Billy," Carrie said softly. "And you know something? He's right, too." She reached up to kiss him softly. He pulled her close, and they lost themselves in the kiss.

"I love you so much," Billy whispered huskily.

"I love you, too," Carrie said. She kissed him again, and it seemed to go on forever, until they heard someone clearing his throat in the doorway.

"Ahem," they heard again. They broke

apart, and looked over at Ian and Becky in the doorway.

"That is, like, so gross," Becky said, folding her arms. "I mean, you could just use the bed, you know."

"Or close the door," Ian added.

Carrie laughed. "I came up here to look for the two of you, actually."

"Why?" Becky asked. "Were you afraid we were doing exactly what you two were just doing?"

"Something like that," Carrie admitted.

"Well, guess again," Ian said. "We were making art. Becky got an idea for a new song, and we needed someplace private to work on it."

"Pres's room?" Carrie guessed.

"The door was open," Becky said defensively. "We didn't touch anything."

"Except each other," Billy said slyly.

"Hey, man, we're artists, okay?" Ian said. "We were making art, like I said."

"Yeah, cool," Billy agreed, trying not to laugh.

"Listen, Ian wrote this incredible song," Becky said to Billy. "It's all about me, actually. And so I was wondering if the Flirts would like to take a look at it."

"Uh, gee—" Billy began.

"Just remember that my band is going to have a cut on the *Sunset Beach Slaughter* soundtrack," Ian reminded him. "We could probably do big things for you."

Billy pretended to think about it. "Well, Ian, I don't think that the Zits and the Flirts do the same kind of tunes, actually."

"But this tune is different," Becky insisted. "It's so cool. It's about *me!* You know, like Crosby, Stills, Nash and Young wrote 'Suite Judy Blue Eyes' about Judy Collins? Or like how Sting did 'Roxanne'? It's about this girl who is, like, so incredible that she breaks this guy's heart and everything."

"Actually, it's a really good song," Carrie admitted. "I read the lyrics."

"Like I said," Becky began. "Ian is—"

"A genius," Carrie said with her.

"Tell you what," Billy said. "I'll look your tune over. But we pretty much only do tunes that the Flirts write, you know?"

"Yeah, cool," Ian argued. "But you'll really look at it?"

"Sure," Billy said.

"Great!" Ian exclaimed. "That's so great! Meet you downstairs, okay?"

"Okay," Billy said. "And close the door on your way out."

"Don't do anything I wouldn't do," Becky said with a smirk.

"Thanks for the tip," Carrie said. "And no detours into Pres's room with the door closed on your way downstairs, okay?"

"Puh-leeze," Becky scoffed, and she dutifully shut the door behind her.

"I was never that young," Carrie said, wrapping her arms around Billy's waist.

"I was," Billy said. "And I would have had Becky back in Pres's room so fast it would make your head spin."

"That's terrible!" Carrie said with a laugh, playfully hitting Billy's arm.

"I thought about girls constantly at that age," Billy said. "Of course, nothing has changed."

She hit him again. "Very funny."

He grabbed her by the waist and pulled her to him. "Actually, I only think about one girl."

"Oh, really?"

"Yes, really," Billy replied.

"Christina?" Carrie asked innocently.

Billy's jaw fell. "My ex?"

Carrie nodded. "She's really beautiful, Billy."

"Yeah," he agreed. "But Christina and I are old news."

"She'd like the old news to be new news again," Carrie said.

"Oh, Carrie, Carrie," Billy said softly. "Don't you know by now? It doesn't matter what she wants. The only girl for me is you. Forever."

"You mean it?"

Billy put one hand under Carrie's knees and another under her back, and he quickly lifted Carrie up into his arms. Gently he carried her to the bed and laid her down on it. Then he lay down next to her and took her into his arms.

"I'm not very good with words sometimes," he said softly. "But there's something I want you to know. I used to wonder about true love, you know? What did that really mean? I used to think that my music was the most important thing in the world to me, and that no girl could ever come first."

Tenderly he pushed some hair off Carrie's face. She gazed up at him, listening.

"But now," Billy continued, "I realize I was wrong. Because you do come first. There is nothing and no one more important to me than you, Carrie. I don't know how I got so lucky, but I'm glad I did."

Carrie gulped hard. "That's just how I feel, too," she whispered, reaching out to touch his face. "You know, when I was trying to decide whether to stay in Seattle with you, I thought I could find answers somewhere else. I even went to some psychics!"

"You?" Billy said with a laugh.

"I know, I was crazy," Carrie admitted. "And then it finally dawned on me that no one could tell me the future, because I had to create my own future. And all the answers were right there inside of me."

"Yeah," Billy agreed. "I know what you mean."

"When you really love someone," Carrie said slowly, "then you want what's best for them. And they want what's best for you, too. And neither of you should have to give up your dreams for the other."

"I never wanted you to give up your dreams, Carrie," Billy said. "I just wanted you with me so badly."

"Sometimes the answer isn't simple, I guess," Carrie admitted. "But maybe there could have been some kind of compromise— like some time in Seattle, and then both of us going to New Haven so I could go back to Yale. Something like that."

Billy nodded thoughtfully. "I'm glad we didn't have to deal with that, though."

"Me, too," Carrie agreed fervently. "But Billy?"

"What?"

"You would be willing to compromise, right?" Carrie asked, searching his eyes.

"Yeah," he said solemnly. "I see that now. My dreams aren't any more or less important than yours, Car."

She wrapped her arms around his neck and squeezed him tight. "You are the coolest, Billy Sampson!"

As she kissed him passionately she dimly heard what sounded like a thundering herd coming up the stairs. The next thing she knew, the entire band, along

206

with Ian and Becky, tumbled into Billy's room.

"Hey!" Billy protested, but he was laughing at the same time. "We could have been getting down in here!"

"That's what we were hoping," Sam said. "You know how I love to live vicariously."

"There's a little somethin' called rehearsal that's supposed to be goin' on," Pres reminded them, leaning against the wall.

"Yeah, and you need to come down and vote about doing my tune," Ian added seriously.

"It's so cool," Becky raved. "I mean it, Ian is—"

"A *genius!*" everyone in the room yelled at the same time.

"Correct," Becky said with dignity. "I'm glad you got the message."

"We'll be down in a few," Billy promised.

"Oh, no you don't," Sam said. She took a flying leap at the bed and landed half on Billy and half on Carrie. "This ought to break up your little love nest."

"Get off me!" Billy protested, cracking up.

"Come one, come all!" Sam called to the group. "If we leave them alone now, we'll never get them downstairs to practice!"

Everyone looked at everyone else, shrugged, and then all together they ran across the room and jumped on Billy's bed.

Which promptly crashed to the floor.

"Oh, great!" Billy yelled. "You broke my bed! You guys are crazy!"

"It's true!" Emma cried gleefully. "We *are* crazy!"

"And we're about to get a recording deal," Jake added, his arm around Erin. "So get your butts downstairs and let's make some music!"

Billy looked at Carrie. "We are seriously outnumbered here," he said.

She nodded. "I guess love will have to take a backseat to music for the moment," she told him.

He leaned close to her and touched her cheek. "Only for the moment," he said softly. "Shall we leave this motley crew with something to talk about?"

"Sure?" Carrie replied. "Why not?"

Then, with the entire group surrounding them on the mattress, which was now on the floor, Billy gave Carrie the most perfect, passionate kiss of her entire life.

And for Carrie everyone disappeared but Billy, and the love that would see them through, come what may.

SUNSET ISLAND MAILBOX

Dear Readers,

As I sit down to write this, we're exactly eight days away from the opening night of my new play, Anne Frank & Me. The mostly teen cast has been working very hard, and the last few nights have been spent hanging and focusing lights, timing sound cues, settling costume changes . . . all the details that make the difference between a great show and an ordinary one.

I think the teens in my cast are working harder than they have in their lives. Yet, no one complains. Because everyone knows that if you're going to be great at something, you have to work extremely hard.

You know from my books that I think the only real failure in life is not to try. Let me add to that: If you're going to try, why not try really, really hard? I believe that every single one of you has a special talent—a talent that sets you apart from everyone else. It might be writing. It might be sports. It might be making jewelry. It might be simply being a terrific, wonderful friend.

Make the most of that talent!

So, what do you think of the summer's

books so far? Should Sam have gone back to live with the Jacobs family again? What can Emma do to make things better with her mother? Should she do anything at all? In this book, did Carrie make the right decision?

Let me know what you think! You know what I think—that my readers are absolutely the coolest, greatest readers any author could ask for. And you know the drill about writing to me . . . every single letter gets an answer!

See you on the island!
Best—
Cherie Bennett

Cherie Bennett
c/o General Licensing Company
24 West 25th Street
New York, New York 10010

All letters printed become property of the publisher.

Dear Cherie,
I'm fourteen years old. My friends and I really, really love your books. I own every one you have written and have read them all about

ten times. *My friend Valli and I are probably the only ones who read your books in Utah.*

> *Sincerely,*
> *Marie Matthews*
> *Millville, Utah*

Dear Marie,

You've read each of my books ten times? That is too cool! There are actually some books that I've read about that many times, like Chaim Potok's The Chosen. Each time I read it, I discover something new. Say hi to Valli for me. Judging from my mail, you are not the only readers in Utah, I promise you!

> Best,
> Cherie

Dear Cherie,

I just finished Sunset Wishes *and I think Carrie was lucky to be in a movie. What is your favorite band? And what is it like in New York?*

> *Sincerely,*
> *Alexandra Hunt*
> *Alberta, Canada*

Dear Alexandra,

I think Carrie was lucky to be in a movie, too, but as you can see, it's a lot of work! Jeff and I just sold a movie based on one of my books. There are a lot of bands that I like. I love the old rock group The Doors; I love the country band Sawyer Brown; and I love the current rock group Arrested Development. As for New York, we liked living there a lot, but we're really happy now to be in Tennessee!

Best,
Cherie

Dear Cherie,
   I'm a relatively new fan, and I just wanted to let you know how fabulous I think your books are. I can't wait until your next one comes out. I think Sam is fantastic (who doesn't?) and I can identify with Carrie, but Emma really irritates me. She pretends to be so detached from her rich life, but, in reality, she's the typical snobby rich girl!
   Sincerely,
   Brittany Stevens
   Peyton, Colorado

Dear Brittany,
   From time to time, each of the characters irritates me, too! Just like real people in the real world. As for Emma, I think once you understand the kind of family she comes from, you'll see that she really is trying to be the best person that she can be. What do you and the other readers think of what's happened to her this summer?

Best,
Cherie

CHERIE BENNETT
BELIEVERS
F A N   C L U B

Hey, Readers! You asked for it, you've got it!

Join your Sunset sisters from all over the world in the greatest fan club in the world...
Cherie Bennett Believers Fan Club!

Here's what you'll get:

★ a personally-autographed-to-you 8x10 glossy photograph of your favorite writer
(I hope!).
★ a bio that answers all those <u>weird questions</u> you always wanted to know, like how
Jeff and I met!
★ a three-times yearly newsletter, telling you <u>everything</u> that's going on in the worlds
of your fave books, and me!
★ a personally-autographed-by-me membership card.
★ an awesome bumper sticker; a locker magnet or mini-notepad.
★ "Sunset Sister" pen pal information that can hook you up with readers all over the
world! Guys, too!
★ and much, much more!

So I say to you – don't delay! Fill out the request form here, clip it, and send it to the
address below, and you'll be rushed fan club information and an enrollment form!

Yes! I'm a Cherie Bennett Believer! Cherie, send me information and an
enrollment form so I can join the **CHERIE BENNETT BELIEVERS FAN CLUB!**

My Name _____

Address _____

Town _____

State/Province _____ Zip _____

Country _____

CHERIE BENNETT BELIEVERS FAN CLUB
P.O. Box 150326
Nashville, Tennessee 37215 USA

items offered may be changed without notice